Jonah's War

by

David Jardine

Order this book online at www.trafford.com
or email orders@trafford.com

Most Trafford titles are also available at major online book retailers.

Note for Librarians: A cataloguing record for this book is available from Library and Archives Canada at www.collectionscanada.ca/amicus/index-e.html

Printed in Victoria, BC, Canada.

ISBN: 978-1-4269-1517-8 (sc)

Our mission is to efficiently provide the world's finest, most comprehensive book publishing service, enabling every author to experience success. To find out how to publish your book, your way, and have it available worldwide, visit us online at www.trafford.com

Trafford rev. 8/13/2009

 www.trafford.com

North America & international
toll-free: 1 888 232 4444 (USA & Canada)
phone: 250 383 6864 ♦ fax: 812 355 4082

FOREWORD

This story springs from an original Civil War diary I discovered amid the discarded junk filling the basement of an old house my wife, Linda, and I bought in 1960. Neatly written in accomplished script with both pen and pencil, the leather-bound, five-by-seven inch journal leapt at me with the sparkle of a discovered diamond. Linda, honest beyond reason it seemed, returned the treasure to its rightful owner, an elderly spinster consigned to an old folks home, but before it escaped I typed an exact copy.

Busy with our careers and three children for the next 30 years, we all but forgot the diary until 1990, when, while moving to the Napa Valley in California, daylight once again illuminated the young soldier's writings. This time I could not let go. The piquant chronicle drew and riveted me as if it were a mythological siren.

Inspired to write something about the soldier, but having learned the value of proper preparation over the years, I read a half-dozen histories of the period and wrote to the National Archives in Washington in search of the soldier's records. To my surprise, the records included copies of his marriage and death certificates, and even gave eyewitness accounts of his woundings. I then traveled to the battlegrounds described in the diary to gain greater insight into the circumstances surrounding his war experiences; at each site copied combat documents and statistics involving him. Now armed and dangerous, I began to feel like an evangelist swept away by his mission, or, more accurately, Richard the Lion-Hearted crusading to free Jerusalem from the clutches of Prince Saladin, thereby emancipating the prince's enslaved people.

As a result of my romantic abandon, this soldier's rather blunt daily entries have given birth to a story of, I hope, greater depth and scope than might otherwise have emerged. I have attempted to make this young man's laconic notations a springboard, catapulting today's reader into the shoes of the men who stood next to this Civil War soldier. But, unfortunately, the process of transcribing original script writing with mechanical tools of necessity eliminates a key factor that often inspires those who read original documents, that is, the emotional connection with the living person who actually held the pen is lost. For example, reading a passage written in the wake of the Shiloh carnage, during Halleck's calculated advance against Beauregard's stubborn Rebels at Corinth, Mississippi, he wrote:

> Tues May 27th [1862] –We went out on picket at 8 a.m. There was skirmishing all day. One man of Company K was killed and two or three wounded in the 32nd Indiana.

And the next day:

> Wed May 28th –We came into camp at 8 a.m. We were called into the entrenchments at noon. There was heavy firing in General Pope and Nelsons and McCooks brigades all day

with heavy musketry. We took two batteries and 160 prisoners.

These entries appear innocuous on the surface. But, damn! I thought when I first read these lines written with his own hand, what could the fellow have been feeling as these events swirled around him? These two entries alone, I believed, could spawn a saga of *Gone With the Wind* magnitude. I fondled the page, knowing his fingers had also touched it. I wanted everyone to somehow make the tactile connection but, since his writings are now beyond reach, it simply cannot be done.

In spite of the twenty-first century printing found here, as our diarist slugs his way into the *Battle of Perryville* (Kentucky), one gains a more solid connection as a result of greater detail. To me, his seemingly cold objectivity is even more evident, masking what must have been overwhelming emotions:

Saturday Oct 4th –Reveille at 4 a.m. and marched at 6. Our regiment [the 26th Ohio Volunteer Infantry] was in the advance. We left the main pike and went by way of Fairfield. When we got within 1 1/2 miles of the fair ground we encamped, but our regiment and the 58th Indiana was sent on ahead. We soon heard heavy musketry in front. We started on in double quick and as we came up to the brow of a hill, our cavalry came back on the run, but when they seen us coming up they rallied again. The artillery ran ahead and our regiment formed a line of battle on the right and sent out skirmishers. After a short cannonading we moved forward and the rebels retreated through Bardstown and left on the Danville pike. We got into town at sundown and encamped in the Catholic church yard. There was great enthusiasm among the citizens where we came in.

So, coupled with the technical impossibility of bringing the soldier's actual hand to this passage, we clearly see here the alarming objectivity that shrouds his lean phraseology throughout, further obfuscating his emotions and diminishing the diary's impact on the modern reader. Even after the Perryville slaughter on October 8 (over 7,500 killed, wounded or missing) his entries continue to lack any trace of passion, in particular the blood-rush of imminent doom one might expect from someone whose life now included a lot of extra lead in the air:

> Saturday Oct 11ᵗʰ, 1862 –While we were eating breakfast the rebels attacked our pickets and came up in sight of camp. Our battery threw a few shell at them and we fell in and marched out and laid in line of battle until 5 p.m.

Neither his zeal nor misery finds its way into this or any other passage, although we know that Civil War soldiers celebrated victories, and the fact that wet, freezing, tormenting weather often plagued and even killed them is common knowledge. Could we be witnessing a Nineteenth Century case of delayed stress disorder? Yet to come was Stones River and Chickamauga, and he fought in the thick of both. Would he stop his robotic descriptions and reveal his common humanity? Well, no, but he must have been as human as any of us today. We can be sure of that.

To his credit, this soldier's matter-of-fact words hold a certain disciplined simplicity, their quiet force sometimes startling me to a standstill, knowing that like an iceberg, eighty-five percent or more of his life lay unseen beneath the surface. At some risk, I have included parts of the submerged in this story, hoping that a blend of diary entry, historical fact and inspired interpretation will not distract the reader.

As casual observers, disconnected from this man by time and space, we cannot know everything he knew, nor feel what he felt after Minié balls tore him up. We can only imagine what this soldier experienced in the War of the Rebellion, and the following is my best guess.

ACKNOWLEDGMENT

The inspiration of my friend, the late Ted Kohler, was of great benefit to me and, through this story, has impacted us all.

DEDICATION

This story is written for my loving wife, Linda, whose strength of character is unmatched, and for our children, Eric, Beth and Alec who, hopefully, found true self-reliance under conditions less violent than those recorded herein.

PREFACE

Like all great wars, the War of the Rebellion was a struggle transcending all other human endeavors of its age, brother against brother, a haunting episode that many contemporary citizens seem to know little about. Hidden from modern America by time and the constantly warping veil of social transformation, it is a monumental example of humankind's unwillingness to admit that its greatest efforts often spring from an act of destruction.

In the beginning, the Federal Army's hasty organization and clumsy tactics reflected an ethnically diverse America still jelling; few imagined that the eclectic mix would achieve the strength it did. And then the struggle became a prolonged, all consuming experience, driving men in lockstep from the epitome of elation to the depths of despair and back again. Further, the widespread effect of the war's cultural surgery still touches the course of American life, notably in geography and politics. Today, the impact the Civil War had across the breadth of society should be telegraphed forward to all succeeding generations.

Early on, the nation's freewheeling expansion needed

freethinking risk-takers, but when the Civil War came along, taking chances while still learning the war business risked more than the money and time one might lose in the commercial world. To make matters worse, our political leaders at the time underestimated the conflict's scope, thereby contributing to the terrible carnage through lack of preparation, a bloodbath that grew exponentially as men struggled to find social and economic justice through combat. And, although military misjudgments became a major ingredient for battlefield disaster, unreliable intelligence networks, bad planning, and outright blundering soon made most Americans aware that the quarrel would not be a limited fight soon forgotten, as they realized after the first *Battle of Bull Run*, which turned out to be only the first battle at Manassas. The war slowly gained momentum, bludgeoning home profound, irreversible social and personal lessons, leaving scars in the flesh of many who survived it, as it did in the case of Jonah Hommen.

At the outset, like most Civil War soldiers, Jonah knew he had become a player in a major historical event, but buried in the ranks he could not know the full scope of the drama as it gathered brawn around him. Information traveled only by horse or wire, frequently became confused, and rumor reigned in the Army of the Ohio as in most armies. Nevertheless, Jonah shunned the unconfirmed speculation and simply kept a factual diary, recording things he actually saw happen. His guileless words, disconnected from us by he weight of one hundred and forty-seven years, obscure his metamorphosis, a wrenching to manhood unnaturally accelerated by the crush of mortal combat.

He died of "excessive bile" at Shawnee County, Kansas, in February, 1891, at the age of 48, having outlived two wives. His funeral attracted little attention, and only those few close friends who lowered his casket knew that his corpse would have been somewhat lighter had it not been for the Rebel ball still embedded in his left thigh.

Jonah and the others, Confederate and Yankee alike, risked their lives for ideas–convictions that underpinned the existence of the very culture that produced them. Ideas like fulfilling the will of God and the nation's manifest destiny, in Jonah's case. The irresistible allure of the heady elixir, one nation under God, as it fermented in Central Ohio and throughout most northern states between 1850 and 1861, proved euphoric for Jonah, a lad baptized in purified mainstream waters. Consequently, he found himself willing to kill fellow humans in order to amputate the Southern cancer. To him, the Dixie cabal had only economic advantage and other mundane goals in mind, not the will of the Maker. But then, the Confederate boys, with their conflicting convictions about the nation's destiny, became homicidal, too.

Young men growing up in the fertile farmlands of Ohio quickly learned that facing off against the welling evil of Southern secession was a birthright that, when the fight started, would bring personal as well as national fulfillment. At Jonah's last church service in Ashley, Ohio, Reverend Sable insisted that those men who volunteered for the army would experience a quintessential fusing of mind, body and spirit as they went to war, punishing sinners to serve God. But for Jonah, the first reality of war meant stepping forward when the 26th Ohio Volunteer Infantry called for men. He did not hesitate.

A sinewy, five foot-ten, eighteen year-old lad with an eighth grade education, he left the family farm for war, taking with him more than the average youth's natural yearning for adventure. He had been sent on a God-blessed mission. But the military's intrinsic tyranny and the escalating conflict accelerated him to age forty by his twenty-first birthday, blurring Reverend Sable's divine ideas in the process.

What was it like? If Jonah were alive today he would undoubtedly falter in an attempt to describe growing up in the Civil War centrifuge. It was too intense, too personal to discuss openly, or even in his private writing. Although his unemotional, daily diary entries record only facts, his understatement screams at us. His chronicle, an archaeological skeleton awaiting examination, has found its moment in history. Here is what happened.

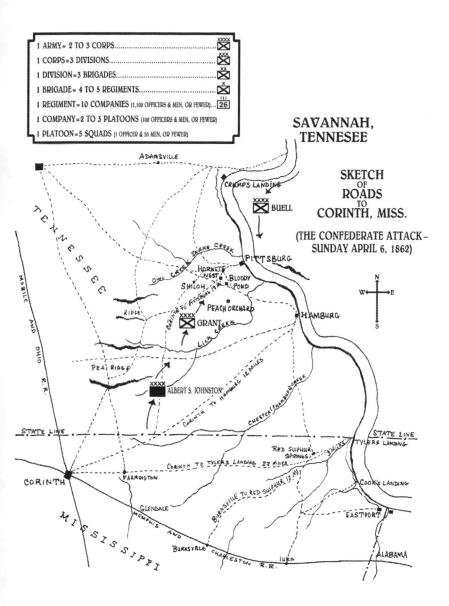

1 ARMY = 2 TO 3 CORPS	XXXX
1 CORPS = 3 DIVISIONS	XXXX
1 DIVISION = 3 BRIGADES	XX
1 BRIGADE = 4 TO 5 REGIMENTS	X
1 REGIMENT = 10 COMPANIES (1,100 OFFICERS & MEN, OR FEWER)	III 26
1 COMPANY = 2 TO 3 PLATOONS (100 OFFICERS & MEN, OR FEWER)	
1 PLATOON = 5 SQUADS (1 OFFICER & 50 MEN, OR FEWER)	

SAVANNAH,
TENNESSEE

SKETCH
OF
ROADS
TO
CORINTH, MISS.

(THE CONFEDERATE ATTACK–
SUNDAY APRIL 6, 1862)

ADAMSVILLE

CRUMPS LANDING

BUELL

TENNESSEE

SNAKE CREEK

OWL CREEK

PITTSBURG

HORNETS
NEST

SHILOH

BLOODY
POND

RIDGE

PEACH ORCHARD

CORINTH TO PITTSBURG 22 MILES

GRANT

LICK CREEK

HAMBURG

N
W   E
S

PEA RIDGE

ALBERT S. JOHNSTON

CORINTH TO HAMBURG 12 MILES

MOBILE AND OHIO R.R.

CHESTER CHURCHING CREEK

STATE LINE

STATE LINE

TYLERS LANDING

RED SULPHUR
SPRINGS

3 MILES

CORINTH TO TYLERS LANDING 22 MILES

COOK'S LANDING

CORINTH

FARMINGTON

BURNSVILLE TO RED SULPHUR 17 MI.

GLENDALE

MEMPHIS AND CHARLESTON R.R.

EASTPORT

MISSISSIPPI

BURNSVILLE CHARLESTON R.R.

IUKA

ALABAMA

1.

"Woe unto you that are full! for ye shall hunger. Woe unto you that laugh now! for ye shall mourn and weep." Luke 6:2

Swollen and muddied from heavy spring rains, the mighty Tennessee River heaved through the woodlands pressing Savannah from the south, a silent witness to the desperate battle raging on her western shore. It was the second and final day of the struggle—Monday, April 7, 1862.

Surging four abreast down the Waynesboro Pike at the quicktime and doublequick, General Don Carlos Buell's Army of the Ohio could only listen to the welling fight beyond Savannah. Tortured by early morning rainsqualls but as yet unscathed by battle, the mass of anxious men boiled forward along the winding road with the unyielding authority of the Tennessee River itself. The land began to rise around them as they advanced toward the river valley, squeezing them from all sides, its glistening, emerald-green hills sending the struggle's relentless cacophony leaping into the columns. Capricious booms and rips cuffed the men with increasing force as they pressed forward, seeming to conspire with the enemy to soften the oncoming Yankee's determination. The Federals broke from the high ground into the lowlands along the river, hearing the rumble of massed cannon shift directly south again then swell to a steady thunder. The distant, mushy rake of a thousand muskets clove the air with fearful slashes.

Private Jonah Hommen of Company C, 26th Ohio Volunteer Infantry, hid his rising apprehension as the Federals poured into the valley and marched, heads up, toward Savannah. But the forty-three men of C Company did not reach the river until sunset, too late to be sent into battle. The company sergeant, Luke Vieland, held muster on the wharf in the waning light.

John Shoemaker, a straggler who had fallen out at Olive Hill suffering a heel blister, snuck from the shadows to find his place in the rear rank just in time to hear his name called. The sergeant saw Shoemaker slinking into place but said nothing. Vieland began to check ammunition pouches as if his men were about to form a line of battle.

"We'll sail upstream on the *Cairo* over thar," Vieland growled, pointing to a steamboat moored fifty yards down the wharf, "and take the bark outta them Secesh dogs."

The exhausted men packed aboard the already crowded boat in the gathering dusk, the last of the 26th finding deck space just as darkness descended with the finality of a dropped stage curtain. The ship's pilot, lantern in hand, called from the bridge to Captain Meredith, C Company's commander, announcing that the vessel could not safely navigate the Tennessee's treacherous waters at night. Not knowing whether they had been rebuked or reprieved, the soldiers stood in the blackness, listening to the dying rattle of cannon upriver. Realizing that they were going nowhere, the men began to settle on the steamer's dew-damp decks, at the same time contemplating the thud of distant Federal gunboats, taking up where the field artillery had left off. Random whispers and coughs stabbed the chilling air. Few slept soundly.

. . . . .

Cairo slipped her moorings at first light on Tuesday, April 8, 1862, and headed upriver for Pittsburg Landing, her mixed cargo of green militia and veteran soldiers ready to finish the fight. The boat knifed steadily into the current, propelling her cargo of human flesh against the flow, her bow sending a lingering wake rippling left and right. Her paddlewheel churned angrily, sending a trail of white foam bubbling into the dark water astern. Lining the rail in the gathering light, the men searched the silent river, examining it as if hoping to glimpse the battle's bloated carcass floating past. Within thirty minutes the paddlewheel began to slow, softening its bite. Sergeant Vieland called his troops into ranks along the starboard rail, checked their weapons and equipment then spun around to report to Captain Meredith: "Company C ready for battle, sir," he barked, handing the captain his muster count.

Meredith returned Vieland's salute. "Have the men stand easy, sergeant."

The cargo of soldiers stared into a wall of fog hugging the shoreline as the ship eased toward the landing on the west bank. The warming sunlight began to melt the feathery fog, its fragile veil slowly evaporating to expose equipment and horses packed tightly along a narrow shoal. Clusters of soldiers, most without rifles, huddled in the murky shadow of a twenty-foot high embankment. A palpable pall lay over the clumsy-quiet men along the bank, some idling with blankets drawn over their shoulders, others squatting around smoky campfires. A few looked up to stare deadpan at the *Cairo*. On board, a deck hand hurled a mooring line toward the nearest cluster of men, but no one picked it up. Finally an officer on shore barked an order, and two of his men grabbed the line.

"What're they doin' here, layin' up like this?" Jonah mumbled, thinking aloud. He glanced at Sam Fry, pressing his elbow.

"They ain't organized," Fry whispered. "Whar's their weapons?"

"Why ain't they on the line a battle?" Shoemaker asked without taking his eyes from the huddled mass. No one answered anyone. Sergeant Vieland, behind them, finally spoke.

"Pay no attention to them fellas, boys, looks like they lost thar stomach for the fight…pay 'em no mind."

The gray river haze had lifted completely, bringing home the full force of the survivors' misery; their powder-blackened faces, somber masks cast in grief and despair, told their story. The fresh troops, standing rigid at the rail, had their weapons planted butt-down between their braced legs as if to steady themselves, their wide-eyed stares falling to frowns of disbelief in the ringing silence. Except for a few thumbs stroking musket barrels, and now and then a quick hand fidgeting a forage cap, there was no movement. Suddenly the ship captain's sharp order to the roustabouts broke the spell.

"Run number one forward! Number three aft! Heave around, take in the slack, men!"

The ship's bow slid along the log-laced landing with the new troops still staring at the confused mass of men crowding the river, most realizing that their late arrival was likely the cause of the scene before them. Jonah remembered why they were late…

…When General Buell detached the 26th Infantry from his Army of the Ohio to scout Lawrenceburg early Friday, the diversion had delayed their arrival at Pittsburgh Landing

4

for two days, at least, Jonah calculated. If his regiment had been on time, it could have helped prevent the Union retreat to the river, a battle that they had simply imagined as they racked along the Waynesboro Pike. The fruitless scouting mission had cost precious time, and now, as they quicktimed at port arms down the brow of the *Cairo* in the early morning light, past the empty steamboats *Lexington* and *Tyler*, Jonah suffered a fleeting pang of guilt.

A mounted colonel galloping along the embankment above the 26th Ohio reined to a stop and pumped his flattened palm down, signaling Colonel Fyffe, commander of the 26th, to slow his troops. The columns surged, clutched, and then jolted to a stop, their jangling equipment instantly silent.

"Hit's over, we're too late," a recruit two files behind Jonah piped. Standing steady, his rifle clutched across his chest, Jonah felt a sense of relief follow the young lad's words. Jonah's shallow breathing steadied and deepened. Had the Lawrenceburg scout saved his life? Nothing happens by chance in God's world, he remembered, visualizing Reverend Sable at the pulpit back in Ashley, his black hair flashing silver as his head bobbed in the sunlight flooding through the window behind him. And Jonah heard the preacher's words again–"...in *God's* world," and he heard the preacher's fist thump the pulpit when he uttered the word "*God*," and he watched the man's black hair shoot bolts of reflected light over his flock.

"Maybe it is, maybe it ain't," Shoemaker rasped, glancing sideways at Jonah while he jacked the heel of one boot with the toe of the other, easing the blister bandage cramping his heel.

Shoemaker's steady voice and casual logic evaporated Jonah's sense of relief. Gazing at the embankment, Jonah imagined what might lie beyond it; his emotional retreat began, a desperate self-defense against what might be waiting for him, a chilling detachment. Fatalism, a quick-sprouting seed often flowering among soldiers before battle, began to germinate in his breast.

A rapid, rout-step march for two hundred yards up the muddy roadway leading over the river bluff brought the 26th Ohio face-to-face with a nightmarish scene. The determined columns pushed forward without hesitation, steadily winding their way past mutilated corpses that had been laid in rows alongside the road. Bloated horses, mangled cannon and more knots of blackened faces lay beyond the bodies. Nothing moved except the column of clean reinforcements. An uncanny sadness, a weighty weariness hung in the air, as did the acrid stench of death and burnt powder.

Unlike the leafed out trees and shrubbery along the river, the timber at Grant's last defensive line had been reduced to kindling–cannon shells had mauled the dense woods, cutting huge swaths, leaving only splintered stumps and scattered tangles of shattered tree limbs. Hastily dug earthworks lay strewn with smashed artillery limbers and equipment, disemboweled horses and ignored Rebel corpses. The imagined pain and despair of yesterday's fight brushed the fresh troops as they moved further into the battle's allegorical aftermath. A few Yankee bodies still lay in the watery trenches, half buried in the sucking mud. While the fresh men riveted on their dead comrades, the unforgettable smell of freshly dug earth, pulverized wood and rotting flesh haunted them.

Glancing from one ghastly spectacle to the next, Jonah struggled to devise a mental shield against what lay around him. The battle's horror could not be denied; the stunning reality left him lightheaded. He knew he must somehow quell his emotional turmoil, and in his desperation, again nursed the idea that this nightmare had been preordained by God. Using the armor of God's grace, Jonah would deflect war's horrors, thereby preserving his strength to deal with it later, when the world became sane.

For twenty minutes the replacement troops wound their way south on the debris-tangled trace toward the now quiet front line, their equipment racking a syncopated accent to their rhythmic thumping. One mile south of Pittsburgh Landing they came to a small pond where Captain Meredith, mounted, raised his arm, halting his company.

"Take a break, First Sergeant," he called to Vieland, "keep 'em close." The men fell out in silence.

Jonah stepped to a splintered tree stump and sank to his knees, shrugging off his knapsack and bedroll then leaning them against the stump. He sat with his back against the pack, his new Springfield rifle-musket lying across his outstretched legs. Bringing up his canteen, he sucked a mouthful, holding steady on the pond across the trail. Four men were busy recovering muddied bodies from the water's edge, carrying the dead to the roadway by their hands and feet.

"Bloody Pond over thar," mumbled Sergeant Vieland, standing behind Jonah. "Hurt men get thirsty real quick. That's why they's there, wounded and went fer water."

Fumbling his canteen back to his side, Jonah stayed fixed on the pond. He saw every detail. The morning sunlight seemed to disappear into the dark water as if sucked inside it, the murky liquid locking in the light like blackberry jelly swallowing a firefly. He glimpsed a crippled skunk, a cub, limping from a crushed sumac thicket. The animal struggled to the inky water, hesitated at the brink, darted its head left and right then began licking its bloody front paw. Its black and white coat shimmered to silver in the rising light. Nosing the water, the cub shied from its own rippling image, then spun around and scampered on three legs back into the undergrowth.

Jonah gazed down the trail to a stand of rain-damp tree

trunks, ebony fingers pointing toward the heavens, their limbs severed as if by an axe. A few untouched trees stood as if nothing had happened, one showing white scars where chunks of bark had been stripped away by screaming balls. A mature maple guarding a shallow swale to his left had survived the cannons' steel scythe, as well as the raking musket fire.

The 7th Indiana Infantry trooped past, followed by the 3rd Ohio Cavalry, breaking the eerie silence surrounding the bloody pond with their syncopated thumping and thudding and clanging, down the muddy trail heading south. Both units had been on the Lawrenceburg scout with the 26th. Staccato snorts from the cavalry's horses quickly faded into the decimated forest. The silence once again descended.

Jonah watched Union stragglers wander up and down the trail, some without weapons, their incessant, darting glances fending off the stares of the resting soldiers.

Suddenly a mounted staff officer reined to a stop and called to Captain Meredith, standing at the pond. The two men advanced on each other, meeting just beyond the road in front of Jonah. The lieutenant dismounted and they shook hands.

"Secesh General Johnston got killed at the peach orchard, just south, John," the lieutenant said, smiling.

"I heard, Peter," Meredith answered. "Did you know General Prentiss got captured?" Meredith asked. "They struck the 53rd Ohio first, but Prentiss held, then got surrounded. I heard it at Savannah headquarters."

"He had the 5th Ohio Battery, isn't that right?"

"That's right, Peter."

"I wonder what happened to Captain Hickenlooper?"

"Andrew? I don't know. I don't know what happened to any of them…the 77th, the 57th…I just don't know."

Although the officers' conversation meant little to Jonah, their rational manners and confident voices did. The two men were calm, collected, as if part of a prosaic scene, somehow disconnected from the world at their feet. The lieutenant shook Captain Meredith's hand and left.

Drawn to a Rebel corpse that had been dragged from the pond and laid next to the road, Jonah began a spontaneous, compulsive examination of the body, like a pathologist searching for a clue that might reveal the cause of death. The man's coat and shirt had been torn open and his white stomach bulged upward, but there was no wound. His death, Jonah concluded, could have begun with a fatal error, maybe something internal, a decision that could not be seen.

Three Federal soldiers stumbled backward through the bushes behind the pond, each dragging a Rebel clad in homespun gray. They heaved the bodies next to the cadaver already lying at the road. They had no wounds. Somehow they did not look dead, just frightened. Jonah stared at the corpses, watching for a sign of life, a twitch, a blink. Were they really dead, dead like David Taylor was back on the twenty-fifth of February, on the march from Camp George Wood to Bowling Green? Unlike these men, David looked dead, lying in the mud, nearly buried by the sticky mire before he even cooled.

Suddenly, above the Rebel bodies, small, white patches of fog, silver balls of vapor, formed in the thin air and began glowing in the sunlight. Abruptly the hovering apparitions swirled, shimmered and swept away in a brilliant flash, like a school of ghostly minnows dissolving in the warm sunshine. Jonah's lips parted. The finality of it, the absolute chasm between the quick and the dead struck him like a blow. He knew then that the soldiers were no longer a part of mankind. They had broken from the main forever, clods of fertile soil dissolved into the infinite sea. But did they die because they were rootless clumps from the beginning, without strong ties to the word of God? Jonah found comfort in the sense of the idea.

A buckboard loaded with captured Secesh weapons—shotguns, hunting rifles and pistols of all types—creaked to a halt back up the trail. Jonah watched a corporal tie the reins to the wheel brake and leap down, picking up a Mississippi Rifle, capped, cocked and ready. He inspected it, snapped the cap away and knocked the barrel against a rock. Jonah counted three unfired balls as they rolled out. Reloading without firing is a sign of fear and panic, Sergeant Vieland had warned, but it was a battle fear Jonah had not felt, a panic he could scarcely imagine. He had buried his quiet terror deep in his bowels and his mind floated like flotsam on the tide, beyond the grasp of his repressed fears' cunning authority.

Trained by tough veterans who had survived battles in the East, Jonah felt confident he would not let confusion in the fight overcome him. He would know what to do when the time came, would not let a panic-jammed weapon cause his death.

He watched two apathetic men carry yet another dead Rebel from the decimated woods and toss the corpse on the pile. Had the man died because he had made a mistake? If the man had been mentally right, morally right and trained right, surely he would not be dead.

Hammering both sides of the age-old conflict between free will and determinism, Jonah again clutched at the refuge that fatalism might offer. Just do the right thing, he finally concluded, and let God decide outcomes, as Reverend Sable had preached. Jonah pictured the reverend's fist hitting the pulpit in emphasis, his black hair sparkling in the Sunday morning light, his eyes of fire....

..."God (thump) has a plan for his children! God (thump) has a plan for our country! This nation will never fulfill its heavenly promise by immoral means. Those who countenance our nation's dissolution will soon be set right.

"Bondage is a *de facto* violation of our sacred Declaration of Independence! It might, my brethren, become necessary to spill blood in God's (thump) name!" With the thunder from Sable at his pulpit ringing in his ears, Jonah once again lifted himself above the battlefield's staggering horror.

Sergeant Vieland barked Company C into ranks by threes and they moved out to his deliberate cadence. The heel-sucking mud quickly made it impossible for coordinated marching. Vieland rattled "Route step" and the men snaked to the sides of the trail.

Jonah glimpsed the faces behind him—Shotwell, Fry, Dorman, Cole, Shoemaker, Ashburn. Unlike the stragglers at Bloody Pond, these men had steady, fearless eyes. The trepidation Jonah had seen in his companions as they filed from the riverboat had vanished, and now, somehow transformed during their rest at the pond, they all seemed part of a determined, unified force. Jonah felt the spirit of their combined strength flow into him, just as Reverend Sable's Godly message had.

The 26th Ohio Volunteers wound their way four miles south to the Spain Branch of Lick Creek, on the heels of the main body of General Buell's Army of the Ohio. Crossing the waist-deep Spain Branch, they moved into an open pasture where three large white tents, Union hospital wall-tents, had been pitched along the far side. In front of the tents, rows of men lay on stretchers in the open field, waiting their turn on the surgeons' tables. The regiment's rumbling wagons, wheezing horses and clanking mess gear did not shield the fresh troops from the anguished cries of the wounded. Soon only the most piercing wails could be heard, the clatter of equipment once again announcing the authority of determined soldiers on the march. The 26th Ohio Volunteers, obedient to the strength of their mass, had found courage in their walk through war's aftermath.

At mid-afternoon the 26th settled on the right flank

of Buell's assembled army, within sight of Grant's troops, and made camp in a grassy field sloping up to dense woods covering the high ground to the south. At five o'clock Captain Meredith ordered Company C out on picket for the night. Combined with other units, the company formed a thin, advanced line scattered along the timbered ridge facing south, ready to warn the main body of a sudden enemy counterattack.

Standing at his assigned position in the April twilight, Jonah studied the terrain on all sides, making sure that he would be familiar with it when it got dark. He then sat down on the thick carpet of spring grass and scanned the small meadow lying just beyond the ridge. Stretching out on his stomach, he glanced left at John Shoemaker then right at Sam Fry, propped himself on his elbow and once again checked the darkening woods behind him. He shrugged off his knapsack, resting his rifle-musket in the crook of his arms just under his chin. Sucking a quick breath, he reached around and spun his belted ammunition pouch, heavy with forty Minié balls and cartridges, to the soft grass, then laid his rifle in front of him. Doffing his forage cap, he brought up his haversack, methodically eating a full day's allowance. Jerky and bread. Two days' rations left.

After supper, Jonah brought his Springfield to his side and rolled onto his back. In the fading western sky a crow circled, black and free, its plumage flashing silver, shimmering in the lingering glow just above the horizon.

Darkness would arrive later every day now as the sun slowly worked its way up from the equator to the Tropic of Cancer. Until June's summer solstice arrived, the days would be getting longer, increasing chances to confront the Secesh. Jonah's eyelids fluttered and finally batted their way closed, and his mind, numb from the emotional weight of the day, began to collapse.

Earlier, on the way to the picket line, John Shoemaker

had said that the Secesh went back to where they came from, Corinth, Mississippi, less than twenty miles south. Jonah quietly wished the Rebels might have retreated even farther, but his brains were spent, and he was not sure exactly what he wished for. He finally slept.

While Jonah Hommen lay on the picket line, newsmen galloped to the nearest telegraph stations. Their estimates of Union losses suffered at *The Battle of Shiloh Church* shocked the nation. The New York *Tribune* reported that General Ulysses S. Grant, commander of the Army of the Tennessee, had felt the wrath of General Henry Halleck, his boss in Washington, for the near defeat. Halleck's criticism centered on Grant's failure to detect Rebel Generals Johnston and Beauregard's advance from Corinth, Mississippi. The late arrival, as yet unexplained, of General Don Carlos Buell was also under fire from Washington. But Jonah cared nothing about fire from Washington, what mattered to him was fire from the Rebels in front.

. . . . .

Relevant Diary Entries

Sunday April 6th
We started on the march at sunrise we heard cannonading from 9 A.M. until dark. We passed through Waynesboro at 10 A.M. We marched 22 miles.

Mond Apr 7th
We had reveille at 1 ½ A.M. but rains prevented us from marching until daylight. We heard cannonading until 3 P.M. We reached Savannah after dark and laid on a steamboat.

Tues Apr 8th
We went up to Pittsburg Landing early in the morning

and encamped 4 miles from the landing. Our Co was on picket.

Wed Apr 9th 62
The company was relieved at noon and we came to camp. There was a flag of truce came to our post while on picket.

Thurs April 10th
We were formed in line of battle at 4 A.M. and stood there until daylight. The long roll beat at 11 ½ A.M. We formed a line of battle and remained until 3 P.M. Our brigade went on picket at sundown.

. . . . .

Brigadier General Thomas J. Wood's Report on Shiloh

(Official Record, Vol X, Part 1, Serial 10)

HDQRS SIXTH DIVISION, ARMY OF THE OHIO.
On the Battle-field, near Pittsburg, Tenn., April 10, 1862

SIR: [General U. S. Grant] I have the honor to submit the following report of the operations of my division in the battle of the 7th instant:

…The Fifteenth Brigade (Brigadier-General Hascall's) was detached [The 26th Ohio Volunteer Infantry was part of the 15th Brigade] by an order of the general commanding, three days' march from the Tennessee River, to make a detour by the way of Lawrence-burg, which prevented it, notwithstanding it made a rapid and laborious forced march, from arriving on the battle-field until 10 o'clock on Tuesday morning. Worn as it then was, it was anxious to participate in the forced reconnaissance. The troops under fire behaved with great coolness and were eager to engage the enemy. The cheerfulness and alacrity with which they bore the labor and fatigue of rapid march, compactly conducted, of 140 miles, from Nashville to Savannah, is an earnest of their zeal to be present in the great battle and victory, and I take great pleasure in commending their soldierly conduct, as well on the march as in the action, to the notice of the commanding general...

I am, sir, very respectfully, your obedient servant,
TH. J. WOOD,
Brigadier-General of Volunteers, Commanding.

2.

"...that thou mightest know the certainty of those things, wherein thou has been instructed." Luke 1:4

It angered Jonah when his father, Harold Hommen, forbid him to volunteer after the first call to arms sounded in Delaware County, Ohio, in April, 1861. Jonah's unvoiced resentment smoldered as he tried to reason his father's decision. A pious man, Harold Hommen nearly worshipped Reverend Sable, who blessed the Northern Cause at every opportunity. Papa always brightened when Weld's Apostles came up from Columbus once a month to preach about the righteousness of the Great Cause. It certainly was not the elder Hommen's religion, but no one, including his wife, dared ask why he would not allow his son to join God's army. Maybe it was because Jonah would not turn eighteen until August. But his father, a man of few words, never explained his reasons.

Then on July 15, Jonah's mother, Martha, found her husband lying in the woodshed, chicken droppings smeared over his knees, pine chips in his hair and an axe in his hand. Although he had gone for firewood only twenty minutes earlier, his face had already turned deep purple by the time she discovered his body. Three days after the burial, the second call to arms sounded, and Jonah was first in line.

But, alas, Martha insisted on her son's deferment so he could help harvest the fall corn, beans and alfalfa, fill the hay loft and fatten the stock for the winter market. Jonah helped his mother and his sister, Sarah, get ready for winter, missing the opportunity to go east with the regiment when they left for the Virginia hill country that summer. Then in January, 1862, Cousin Ben and Uncle Seth, Papa Hommen's brother, came from Chicago to work the farm for Mother Martha and Sister Sarah, not a minute too soon.

Eager as a suckling calf, Jonah finally started out for his regiment on Monday, February 17, having heard a rumor that the 26th Ohio was camped at Mumfordsville, Kentucky. The entire family stood on the front porch waving him out of sight, his normally stoic mother unable to check her tears. But Uncle Seth, a man of compassion, provided Martha comfort by warming her waist with his muscled arm as they watched Jonah disappear down the road.

Jonah walked two miles east to Ashley where he caught a ride in neighbor Pardee's wagon, all the way to Columbus. For fifty cents, freight rate for army men, Jonah rode southwest on the railway cars to Cincinnati, arriving at noon Tuesday. Nearly running to the docks, Jonah soared up the brow of the steamer *Major Anderson*, bound down the great Ohio River for Louisville. He delivered his military order into the gnarled hand of the purser, who took out a pen and wrote "free passage" on the back of the paper. Standing at the rail waiting to get underway, Jonah watched passengers, including pretty women dressed in the latest fashion, stroll aboard and wander the decks, but everyone ran for cover when the rain started.

Not wanting to miss anything, Jonah unrolled his oilcloth poncho and stayed on deck, even though the winter drizzle drove a chill to his bones. He stood gripping the rail, soaking up the view and the rain as it leaked through his new straw hat and down his neck. A young man wearing a canvas raincoat stepped alongside him.

"Name's John Ashburn," the stranger announced. They shook hands, both impressed by the grip of the other.

"Jonah Hommen. Headed for the 26th Ohio."

"That so? So am I."

They turned back to the river.

"The Ohio always humbles me, the power of it," Ashburn said.

"It looks alive, almost," Jonah breathed, "rollin' along tryin' ta get somewheres, do somethin' big, like us, maybe."

"She don't give two shucks 'bout nothin', Jonah, not even the *Major Anderson,* under our feet here. When she swells, like she is now, this ship's nothin' but a sparrow ridin' the back of a bull."

As the *Major Anderson* slipped her moorings, the two walked toward the stern to watch the paddle wheel kick up a boil. Jonah traced the ship's wake, a ribbon of white foam trailing off astern, quickly swallowed by the hungry, dark water.

"Yer first time on the river, Jonah?"

"Yessir. I didn't think it would be so big an' powerful."

"I'm from Hamilton County," Ashburn mumbled, "I seen it plenty."

They looked left to see the shoreline suddenly coming at them, getting too close it seemed, but the ship suddenly changed course and the land faded away, then a dark curtain of rain swallowed it in a single gulp.

"I hope whoever's steerin' this boat knows what they're doin'," Jonah said.

"Sure they do," Ashburn answered, "If we can't trust the captain, who can we trust?"

In mid-afternoon the rain stopped and both banks came

into view, revealing stands of naked trees, wet, black and still. The timber hugged the shoreline, guiding the powerful river through the countryside, and the water seethed against the land, unwilling to submit to its authority, relentlessly attacking its muddy banks, swallowing its arrogant enemy chunk by chunk. Jonah watched the battle rage left and right. A hand thumped his shoulder and he spun around.

"Say lad, where are you headed?" the thumper asked, smiling.

"My outfit, the 26ᵗʰ Ohio…they're at Mumfordsville, I hear," Jonah answered, watching three more men come out of the deckhouse, all looking straight at him.

"Well then, we're all headed in the same direction… in the same boat, so to speak!" the big man boomed, "since we're all volunteered to the 26ᵗʰ Ohio. I'm Hicks, this is Shotwell," he said, pointing to the first man behind him, and nodding at the others as he introduced them. "This is Dorman and Bradfield. I see you met Ashburn." The strangers shook hands, a formal thing, but a ritual allowing one to judge the confidence of the other, according to the force of the grip. Jonah made his handshake firm, with extra linger.

"We got to Cincinnati yesterday," Hicks continued. "Did you just arrive in town? Where are you from?" Before he could answer, Dorman suggested that they find the kitchen and a pot of coffee.

Everyone except Ashburn came from either Delaware or Marion County, and had either known or heard of the others' families. Jonah learned that Hicks had received captain's papers from Governor Dennison the week before. The six men left the kitchen to settle on whiskey kegs and straw bales under the fantail awning, steaming mugs in hand.

"I figgered I was the only straggler," Jonah said, blowing on his coffee.

"None of us is a straggler, they're building up the regiment," Hicks explained.

"I didn't know hit got tore down," Dorman countered, smiling. Bradfield pointed a finger at Dorman.

"Hit ain't, leastwise not until *you* get thar," he said, punching Dorman's shoulder.

The ship moored at the Louisville quay after dark, where the men, bowing to the judgment of Captain Hicks, slept in the steamer's hold. At first light the next morning they folded their blankets, returned them to the quartermaster and went ashore to find breakfast.

Hicks told them that his friend, Colonel Edward Pierce Fyffe, would be at the National Hotel, "which surely must have a kitchen," he added. They quickly found the National and the colonel, sitting at a table in the hotel barroom eating a steak and eggs breakfast. Jonah recognized Colonel Fyffe as soon as he saw him, remembering that he was a solid citizen of good reputation who had once sold a saddle to his father back in Ashley. Hicks had mentioned that Colonel Fyffe might be commanding the whole regiment, and that made sense to Jonah, since his father had said the man was college educated and respected by all. The colonel invited them to join him.

After eating ham, potatoes and toasted rye bread, Jonah and John Ashburn left the hotel to see Louisville, but spent much of the morning in a dry goods store, hiding from one freezing rain squall after another.

Dark, scuttling clouds spat rain all afternoon, which began to turn the streets to ice. Unable to find transportation, the volunteers pooled their money and rented two rooms at the National, Hicks donating most of the money. The next morning they went to Colonel Fyffe's room where an aged doctor, a pince-nez gripping his nose and a towel gripping his neck, answered their knock.

"The colonel's sick, fellas, influenza…he said you should

go on. Which one of you is Hicks?"

Hicks nodded.

"The colonel says that he recognizes your captaincy, and puts you in charge."

They ate molasses-laced beans, scrambled eggs and buttered bread in the barroom, then Captain Hicks found a railway agent and got his charges government passes for general boarding on the cars, and they headed south.

Five hours later, Mumfordsville's depot slid to a stop alongside the train, and the men scrambled onto the loading platform. The train left before they could find anyone who knew where the 26th might be located.

"The 65th Ohio's bivouacked two mile down Hardyville Road, thataway," the stationmaster said, pointing. Captain Hicks thanked him, and they hiked east in the mud, hoping that the 65th might have extra rations and dry sleeping straw.

While using the latrine at the 65th, Jonah met Mort James and Cyrins Clark from Jefferson County, who graciously offered to share their fire with him. After a fresh rabbit stew supper, Mort and Cyrins showed Jonah their government issued rifle-muskets and ammunition. Fascinated, Jonah watched them demonstrate close-order drill with the weapons, and as they did he realized that he was still not yet a part of the authentic army.

"Guess they'll loan me a gun when I get thar," he mumbled.

"Sure they will," the two chorused, caught up in their veteran status.

Mort snapped the bayonet from his gun's barrel and handed it to Jonah. "Try a throw," he said, beaming.

The knife had a nice balance, a solid feel. They watched Jonah throw, sticking the blade dead center in a live oak twenty paces away.

"Damn, you got a arm!" Cyrins exploded.

"Take game with a knife now and again when the powder gets too damp," Jonah said, smiling.

The 65th marched east at first light but the six men headed north, albeit a rumored direction, chasing their regiment. Bradfield worried that the war might end before they could find their outfit.

"I heard at headquarters that the boys are camped on the Green River," Captain Hicks said, "but no one knew exactly where." When they got to the river, a farmer named Winslow said the soldiers had left that morning, heading west. The men stayed overnight at the Winslow farm and did not catch up to their regiment until late Saturday, the twenty-second of February 1862. As soon as he saw the bivouac fires and the regimental flag flying above the command tent, six months after enlisting, Jonah knew that he was a soldier at last.

He signed the muster roll on a table in front of the headquarters tent the next morning, and was immediately issued a belt and cartridge case, haversack, blanket and uniform from a row of supply wagons. The quartermaster insisted that he burn his civilian blanket because of a lice scare, then go to the ordnance tent for weapons issue.

The recruits carried their new gear to a grove of trees behind the quartermaster's wagons. From his new haversack, Jonah removed the black leather belt with a matching cartridge box looped on it. The brass belt buckle had a raised spread-eagle covering the face of it. His new trappings seemed to possess a magical quality, Federal official, Old Testament solid.

Fresh from the factory, his uniform smelled as new as the yard goods display on the counter at Overmeiers' Mercantile back in Ashley. The five recruits stripped and put on their uniforms.

"Seems a mite scratchy," Dorman complained.

"Mine's like corn silk 'cross a baby's butt," Bradfield

countered.

"Sure it does. You got the hide of a buffalo."

"An' you got the skin of a whelped mouse."

The warm wool brought Jonah inexplicable comfort, confirming that he had finally become a soldier. The men bundled their civilian clothing and went to the ordnance tent, as instructed.

On a table outside the tent the men signed for new Springfields and a bayonet knife, just like Mort James had at the 65th.

"She's got a good heft fer throwin'," Jonah told his comrades, teasing his thumb across the blade, "and oughta be good for skinnin' too, after some honin'."

That evening he practiced throwing his bayonet at a plank behind the mess tent. The adjutant stopped to watch. "The way you handle that blade, Private Hommen, you should keep it belted and ready at all times," the major said, "except when you're told to fix it on your weapon, of course."

Captain Hicks went to command Company F, and the recruits were assigned to Company C. Colonel Fyffe took charge of the entire regiment on the first day of March, and Captain Meredith took command of Company C on March fourth. And march forth the recruits did, "like Clydesdales turned loose in the oat field, tramplin' more than they et," according to C Company's First Sergeant, a man named Luke Vieland.

The new men, seen by their first sergeant as a debilitating influence, had no idea what Vieland had in mind when he called them out for special instruction that evening. "Gear and Water on the March Training", he called the lecture, but it turned out to be more than equipment maintenance and water conservation. Vieland warned them that he did not allow his recruits to fraternize with the officers, as they had with Captain Hicks and Colonel Fyffe during their search for the regiment. He quietly explained that being too social with officers could cause trouble in the fight, and that the officers carried swords not only to kill the enemy, but to smack the asses of stragglers. "Social standin' don't figure into the overall calculation no more," he warned.

"But what if ya knows 'em from home anyways?" Dorman muttered, scraping mud from his boot with a stick. The sergeant riveted on him, watching Dorman read his unvoiced answer in his unrelenting stare, then dismissed the men without a word.

Vieland, an average sized man weighing around 160 pounds, looked about 35 years old, somewhat older than most soldiers. But he was mule-kick quick, tough, and had arms and legs as strong as a limber's tongue. He said he came from Marion County, but no one could remember his family. He always spoke softly when addressing an individual, but when he gave orders to the ranks they could hear his distinctive clack a half-mile away. Ignoring the idle palaver of his men, he made no casual remarks, but they quickly learned that if they wanted an official answer to their questions, he was the man to ask.

Vieland's laconic expressions and calculated mien impressed the recruits, giving them immediate confidence. Mild-mannered yet crusty solid, he treated everyone with respect, not simply according to military rank, and he had no favorites.

The sergeant had been with the 26th all through the Virginia Campaign of the previous summer, and before that he had fought in the Mexican War with Tyler and Scott. Rumors about his exploits in Mexico abounded, centering on how he had learned to do things right, from the battle mistakes of his own company sergeant at the time. The object, Vieland once said, was not to die a hero today, but to stay alive to kill more Rebels tomorrow. Let the enemy suffer death if they want to be heroes, not you.

The recruits quickly learned that their sergeant was a man who knew how to plow a rocky field without destroying the plow. Vieland had probably done things the way they should be done all his life, they concluded, and fighting was no exception.

The sergeant's demeanor told most new men not to attempt a frivolous conversation with him. But John Shoemaker, who had joined the company in January, tried once. He said that Vieland told him he would not "jaw" with recruits, since they had not been in the fight and, therefore, could not imagine a good question. Vieland had few words for his greenhorn warriors, other than training commands, always barked in a steady, calculated style:

"Hit the ground—on yer back—load—*roll—fire!*"

He pressed his men like a "coon after carp", according to Shoemaker, day after day, Camp George Wood, Bowling Green, then to Nashville, Franklin, Columbia and Henrysville. It did not matter if they had tramped two miles or twenty-two miles, Vieland insisted that the big fight could come at any time, and they must ready:

"Down—on yer back—load—*roll—fire!*"

On Sunday, March 16, one of the new men accidentally wounded a friend, the ball burning his friend's right shoulder, but neither the careless act nor the temporary casualty seemed to bother Sergeant Vieland. At morning muster he called out the shooter, had him explain his mistake, then said it was a lesson for everyone, and left.

Although Vieland's discipline grew more intense as the regiment marched further south, he never became angry when his recruits first made a mistake. His capacity for patience impressed even the older hands. He showed his new men how to do something once, and from then on he took for granted that the soldier could do it whenever he gave the order. Daily instruction included charging in a straight line, flanking left and right, and bayoneting a man who did not expect it, by the fake and thrust.

Sergeant Vieland never told anyone to do anything he could not do himself. Knowing this, the men did their best, making every effort to gain his approval, which usually came in the form of a twinkling eye. Even after a full day's march, he often called out his recruits for further training. It took a month before they could shoot their weapons to his standards:

"Hit the ground–on yer back–load–*roll–fire! Shoot low!*"

After weapons drill he usually exercised them in keeping themselves spaced properly in a moving skirmish line; he would not allow straggling no matter how rugged the terrain. He did not mind putting muscle behind his words. On one occasion when the company went out on picket, he noticed a man lying at an improper interval, too close to the next man. He snatched the bumpkin's belt and dragged him into position. A bit harsh, a few reasoned, but Vieland's determination to go to any lengths to train his men seemed to help everyone understand the importance of doing things right in order to stay alive.

Dress parade was held on Tuesday the twenty-fifth of March, at which time General Thomas John Wood inspected the regiment. In a speech afterward, he complemented the men on their clean uniforms and marching skills, although he had, no doubt, noticed a few new men who could not keep step, even with a drum beating. The general's praise raised everyone's spirits but, to Jonah, the praise could not hold a candle to a single word, like "good" from Sergeant Vieland.

After the ceremony, Vieland held Company C in formation at the parade ground and told them that General Wood suffered from poor eyesight since the general, apparently, did not see their constant fidgets.

"If you boys can't remember how ta act in front of a

friendly gen'ral, I wonder if you'll hold still when yer waitin' fer the Secesh ta come at yer throats. Glancing over his shoulder toward the reviewing stand he clipped, "I never seed anyone *orate* the enemy ta death."

He dismissed the veterans and marched the recruits to a pile of cobblestones that had been brought up from the creek bed to fill the camp's mud holes, then sent the men, four at a time, to the top of the rocks. After spacing them evenly, he asked Private Cole to go for a cook pot and wagon pin. When the equipment arrived he held the pot behind the men's heads and began beating it with the wagon pin, holding the kettle close so that the pin brushed their ears as he swung. The shooters had to concentrate just to bite off a powder cartridge.

"From the prone–load–*fire!*"

"On yer knees–load–*fire!*"

"On yer back–load–*roll–fire!*"

"Don't jerk the trigger, *squeeze*, damn it! *Shoot low!*" he bellowed between whacks.

Sam Fry, who had joined the company with Shoemaker in January, swore that they would run the regiment out of ammunition before darkness set in. The men, their cheeks blackened by powder flashes, resembled wide-eyed actors on minstrel stage, peering from charcoaled faces in the fading limelight. Afterward, Shoemaker, the mellifluous son of a lawyer, said that he was tired of shooting strung-up straw bags that looked like gunny-sacked fish more than Secesh. "I'm gettin' sick of it, my fellows, to speak the truth," he complained, hitching up his trousers. He had lost another five pounds that week.

Elias Cole, the pin-and-pot fetcher who had been with the company since Christmas, came to the recruits' cookfire that evening. Cole had a reputation as a lad of few words, but that night he took a minute to rumble about the dangers of over-training. He said that Colonel Fyffe's rule requiring them to dig fighting holes and trenches at every bivouac, rain or shine, did nothing but sap what little strength they had left. By the end of March, the romance of army life seemed to have suffered a serious setback.

The men were vaccinated for smallpox on Thursday, March 27, and most became sick, which added medicinal malaise to their training misery. But the sergeant, vaccinated and sick too, refused to let the inoculation interfere with his instruction program. "If yer first lick at 'em misses, that Reb snake'll strike ya dead," he told them, "so yer can't afford to miss nothin'."

The vaccination reaction passed, and on an unusually warm day in early April at Mount Pleasant, Tennessee, Jonah decided to try to speak with his sergeant, a task not easily undertaken. Vieland looked peaceful sitting alone on an empty flour keg, quietly smoking his pipe.

"Sergeant, when you think we might see a Rebel?" Jonah asked, dropping to one knee a few feet from the sergeant.

"Soon."

Vieland looked away, but Jonah, realizing he had asked the wrong question, went to both knees and leaned closer.

"Seems like plenty a work with no end in sight," he said.

"Stickin' with the trainin' takes gumption lad…and there's no glory in it," Vieland whispered, coming around. "But it's the only thing keeps men alive in the fight. Fightin's always a confusin' thing when it happens, but it'll go our way if we do things right, without thinkin'…we got ta have natural instinct reactions, like a fightin' bear, or we won't survive. There's honor in the scrap, 'specially when we win. I never lost. Let's keep it that way, lad. We'll use our trainin' soon enough."

Vieland held steady on Jonah after he spoke, his piercing but kind eyes launching goose bumps on Jonah's forearms. He knew that Sergeant Vieland was a man of honor who would never hesitate to tackle the toughest job, and knowing that, he realized, made every man do his best for him.

Although Sergeant Vieland's discipline seemed unreasonable at times, it had become routine; the men had learned to accept hard marching and drills as a normal part of everyday life. The men had noticed even the officers looking to Vieland for reassurance, occasionally asking him questions in order to make the right decisions. A synergistic mix of strength and humility, Vieland had an inner calmness that never left him, no matter how tough things seemed to his men. After the flour barrel talk, Jonah swore to himself that, if he had anything to do with it, Sergeant Luke Vieland would never lose.

At reveille formation the next Sunday, after Captain Meredith had taken the muster slip, he announced that they had hanged the slave trader Nathaniel Gordon on Washington's Birthday. The captain told them that General Grant had taken Fort Henry on the Tennessee River and Fort Donelson on the Cumberland, and then moved south. Like Grant, the captain said, their commander, General Buell, would march his Army of the Ohio toward Mississippi, where the Rebels were said to be strong. And sure enough, every day the marching distances got longer and the pace got faster. Things had started to warm up, just like Sergeant Vieland had predicted.

When the regiment came in too late for the fight at Shiloh Church, a few men said they might have missed the war. But later, when two veterans from the 8th Iowa visited their camp, those still holding hope for an early end gave up the idea. The two 8th Iowa veterans had scrapped at what they called the Hornet's Nest, and behind their words lay the weight of terror, something Jonah had yet to face.

. . . . .

David Jardine

Relevant Diary Entries

Monday Feb. 17th 1862
I left Ashley Delaware Co Ohio for the 26th Ohio Regt. – arrived at Columbus at 1 oclock P.M. remained there the rest of the day.

Tues Feb 18th 1862
Started of Cincinati at 2A.M. arrived there at 7 A.M. got aboard the steamer Major Anderson and started for Louisville at 12 M. arrived there at 11 P.M.

Wed Feb 19.
I went ashore at 7 a.m. in company with Capt Hicks B. W. shotwell, E. V. Dorman Jas Bradfield and Jas Nugent and went up at the National Hotel. It snowed and rained all day. We found Col. Fyffe at the Hotel.

Thurs Feb 20th 62
We took the cars for Mumfordsville at 7 a.m. where we arrived at 5 P.M. I staid with the 65th Ohio Regt.

We started early for the Regt encamped on Green river we went there and found the Regt had marched for Mumfordsville. We traveled until dark and stoped at a private house

Sat Feb 22nd
Started on early for the Regt. We caught up at 8 a.m. we marched until noon and encamped at Camp George Wood. Very rainy and muddy.

3.

*"And as ye would that men should do to you, do ye also to
them likewise." Luke 6:31*

The massed armies of Generals Grant and Buell, directed by
cautious General Henry Halleck, crawled toward Corinth,
Mississippi, closely watched by an apprehensive citizenry both
North and South. Sprinkled among the battle tested veterans
were raw recruits, sometimes entire regiments that had merely
tiptoed through Shiloh's leftover gore, as had the 26th Ohio.

Unrelenting advice from Washington, coupled with
General Halleck's circumspect planning, turned the
advance on Corinth, merely a day's march from Shiloh,
into a tedious, two-month dawdle. False starts, strategic
shufflings and fruitless deployments, half-strokes
accomplishing little, gave the well-oiled Federal war
machine the viscosity of blackstrap molasses. Predictably,
the Yankee leadership's rising apprehension found its way
into the rank and file, dogging the Bluecoats' heels as they
thumped the breastworks of determined Dixielanders, now
defending home soil.

General Halleck's piecemeal planning served to deny Jonah Hommen and his comrades a chance to prove themselves. The crawl to Corinth not only fed the untested men's trepidation, it honed their anxiety to a point that rumors became addictive. The fact that Generals Pope, Nelson or McCook's brigades seemed to be always between the 26th and the stubborn Rebels became a mixed blessing.

The men listened to cannonading and skirmish musketry daily, fully aware that the swelling boil in front of them might be the first blister on the next battle's back. But, day after day, the ominous booms and tears brought only more spastic maneuvering and countermarches. Life's reality for the 26th Ohio became the long drum roll sending men scurrying to stagnant battle fronts, muddy skirmish lines, tedious picket duty, inspections, and dress parade twice a week.

On the last day of April, Company C had the added pleasure of providing six men to help dig the regimental latrine. The latrine detail shouldered their shovels and headed into the woods, listening, as usual, to the far-off thud of cannon.

"When's that Secesh polecat comin' outta his hole?" grumbled Shotwell, a lad from Columbus who had been in the army only one month.

"He ain't crawled inta it yet," Shoemaker shot back.

"An' I hope he don't," Jonah added. "He ain't even cornered yet, so why ain't we after him?"

"Hit's the strategy of the thing," Fry mumbled. Shotwell grabbed Fry's arm and spun him around. Everyone stopped.

"Whut strategy, Sam?" Shotwell gushed. "Ya mean lettin' the ratty bastards nibble at us like we was a piece a cheese? That's whut thar a-doin'! Don't ya know we got more men then they got? At least that's what I heard when

32

I was guardin' Fyffe's Sibley yesterday!"

The latrine detail started forward again, this time in silence.

Joining diggers from other units, the six from Company C stood for a moment watching the slit trench take shape. The pungent smell of decaying leaves rose from the turned earth, an odor reminiscent of the Shiloh entrenchments. Jonah stared into the ditch. The wet, black, bottom land seemed almost too sticky for digging. Along the sides, dark roots, scraped and cut by the sharp blades, glistened white in the sunlight. He walked to the end of the trench and began digging.

. . . . .

Knowing that the same furious butchers who had pushed Grant back at Shiloh were waiting only a few miles in front of them, men who had strayed from the church as well as those inclined toward agnosticism experienced a miraculous spiritual awakening. The latter day converts began to swell attendance at religious services. The large gatherings sometimes forced Jonah to stand beyond earshot. But when the sermon ended, he could watch the parson's stern face turn to heaven, no doubt asking God to bless the Union's noble cause.

In spite of church and frequent prayers, Jonah's untried battle backbone began to ache regularly. On Sunday, May 11, self-doubt tightened his chest with a vengeance, so he attended services in both his own regiment and the 17th Indiana Infantry. After breakfast that day he signed the payroll, answered church call, and at ten a.m., after services in the 26th, hiked a half-mile to hear the 17th's chaplain from Terre Haute, Reverend Pomeroy. Determined to preach the benefits of Christianity to the avalanche of latter-day Indiana converts in spite of his broken arm, Pomeroy reeked enthusiasm. In his haste to deliver the word of God the previous Sunday, the preacher had fallen from his horse.

Comfortably warm under the cloudless morning sky, the swelling congregation gathered on the sunbathed hillside in a grassy, five-acre pasture sloping to a dry creek bed. A soft, lilac-scented breeze wafted over the hushed penitents, kindling an air of expectation. The pastoral scene and complaisant audience reminded Jonah of a sketch he had seen in a hymnal, a rustic Galilee setting with Christ in the center, his arms raised toward heaven, a sanctuary, Jonah guessed, that the soldier suppliants surrounding him feared they might visit all too soon.

Parson Pomeroy left no doubt about the righteousness of the Union's struggle, calling it "An armed crusade sanctioned by God to bring justice to those who would ignore His will." The preacher's certainty of purpose reassured Jonah, confirming his conviction that the war, in God's eyes, ranked higher than even the early Christian Crusades.

The Terre Haute preacher's eloquent speech unfolded with the irrefutable logic of Reverend Sable; Pomeroy's black hair flashed in the morning sunlight just like Sable's, his fiery eyes triggering the Sable glint. The preacher distilled religion and The Cause into one tantalizing nectar, and once again Jonah felt the magic that had touched him when Weld's Apostles pled for unity of purpose among the citizens of Ashley. But when Jonah returned to his tent after church, the confidence he had felt during the sermon in the sun had spun away, lost in the rumble of distant cannon.

The next day, desperate for relief from his mounting anxiety once again, he began sniffing around the veteran soldiers from other units, the confident-looking men, searching for the key to their inner strength. The intrepid veterans looked the way he wanted to feel. He longed to be one of them. But, seemingly reluctant to make friends, the experienced soldiers paid him little attention.

As the Federals inched south, the bugle's routine call to assembly grew more burdensome than the din of distant cannon. The officers, Shoemaker explained, had decided that parades and inspections kept discipline alive, which, they believed, would enhance confidence. Shoemaker's explanation of camp life did little to mitigate Jonah's anxiety.

"You think there's a Secesh spy a-watchin' us," Fry muttered, addressing thin air as they marched past the reviewing stand in a drizzling rain. "Makin' notes," he added when they had cleared the row of reviewing officers, "on our close-order drill so's the Rebs can attack without bein' crushed ta death under our feet?"

"There ain't no escapin' the deadly Yankee stomp," Shoemaker honked. Although Jonah found some relief in the humor of his friends, he found himself unable to vent his own emotional distress through drollery.

At times, his comrades seemed desperate to divert their anxiety. During supper one evening, Shoemaker, after having cracked a tooth on buckshot, found his beans and molasses laced with the lead pellets. He retaliated by kneading horsehair into smoking tobacco and passing tainted mixture out to whoever might take it. Such harmful diversions began to make Jonah even more anxious.

On Tuesday, May 13, Jonah asked Sergeant Vieland if he could visit his friends, Mort James and Cyrins Clark in the 65th Ohio. It was an unusually quiet afternoon, and the 65th had made camp only a half-mile north.

"We laid on our arms last night," Vieland clipped, "and we'll do the same tonight. Did ya know we found sign that the Rebs crawled inta the brush straightaway in front of ya, when you were on picket yesterday?"

"No, was...?"

"Only twenty rods from yer nose, Private Hommen, and they hid thar fer some time, it looked like. Ya can go, but listen fer the drum roll. On any 'count, be back afore dark."

"I will, Sergeant."

Vieland smiled, locked on Jonah's eyes and whispered: "Ya don't need help from the others to find yerself, lad. It'll come on its own, in the fight."

When Jonah reached the 65th, he discovered that Mort James and Cyrins Clark had been sent to guard their regimental headquarters and could not have visitors. On the way back, he was surprised to find the 45th Illinois setting up camp in a wide, wooded draw. In D Company of the 45th he found his cousins, William and Amos, sons of Uncle Seth, the brothers having just arrived from Chicago. William introduced him to a man who had been in the Shiloh fight, and in his pithy words Jonah heard the casehardened wisdom of a veteran soldier.

"Our first sergeant," Jonah murmured, "says a man has ta have instincts in battle like a fightin' animal. No time fer thinkin'. That how you see it?"

The soldier simply nodded. Jonah saw certainty in the veteran's eyes, an inner strength, telling him that the man had found the answer to self-doubt, the monster that had hounded Jonah since Shiloh.

Jonah learned that nearly all the men of the 45th Illinois had fought at Shiloh. He watched them closely. They reminded him of confessed sinners rising from ossified knees, humbled and strengthened by their deliverance from the gates of hell. But the veteran friend of his cousin had nothing to say about religion or God, even when Jonah asked about church services in the 45th. The man stared at him, quietly exuding the confidence Jonah had grown desperate to possess, and the frustration of not being able to divine the source of the battle veteran's inner strength began to overwhelm him.

By mid-May, with the Mississippi state line at their backs and the Confederates consolidating their defenses in front of Corinth, the Federals heard massed cannon rumble all day long. In spite of the shelling just ahead, the routine of Company C remained unchanged–days laced with marching drills, inspections and parades, evenings adrift in the ebb and flow of strained silences. When sundown stilled the distant thunder, the soldiers gathered around their scattered campfires like reprieved prisoners.

On the evening of May 20, a Tuesday wasted running from one breastwork to another with little rest, John Shoemaker, Elias Cole and Jonah lazed around their timid little cookfire, each man anxious to put away the day's ambivalence in his own way. They spoke not to each other but to the dying flames, watching the embers gasp and pant as if the tension-laced air were choking them.

"Ya know," Cole drawled, "I think the vet'rans did some things in the fight they won't admit to. They whomped the Rebs up north, but now they won't fess up to shootin' nobody. Who the hell killed all them Secesh we saw?"

A diminutive but wiry rascal, Elias Cole was the product of a hired hand and his unschooled wife back in Licking County, the poorest of the poor, and had to be told when to shave, which happened every third or fourth day. Although an infrequent nod was usually the only sign of mental activity, his friends soon learned that there was plenty of undetected activity going on. In spite of his withdrawn manner, he enjoyed the company of his few friends. Being relaxed and low-key by nature, Cole rarely touched off a conversation; his unprovoked soliloquy drew everyone's attention.

"I know they did more than they're sayin'!" Shoemaker yelped, delighted that Cole had swung open the gate, letting out the horse everyone wanted to rope. He shot

Cole a swift glance. "When a man's cornered, he always does more'n he thinks he can, and he never knows what he done 'till he's had a chance to think things through. Yep, and the trick is to learn somethin' from it…make the thing a learnin' lesson."

John Shoemaker, an alert youth with bugle-call volume, had inherited his father's knack for polishing hazy details. Father Seymore Shoemaker practiced law in Columbus, Ohio, where, after Fort Sumter, his editorializing about the Union's imminent success found its way into the *Columbus Journal* more often than did Abraham Lincoln commentary. Private Shoemaker's solid, six-foot frame dominated most situations, but since he left home against his father's will, the lad had lost twenty-five pounds. His uniform, a size too large now, hung loosely from his broad shoulders.

"Yep, but the trick is ta live long 'nough ta learn somethin' from it," Jonah puffed, adding a belated chuckle hinting of his uncertainty. Although his mental stratagems had rescued his psyche during the stroll through Shiloh's carnage, his brain game would not work in the long run, and he had begun to realize it. His emotional defenses had worn thin on the march south—he desperately needed the support of his friends. "From the looks a Shiloh," he went on, watching the gray, curling smoke hesitate under the canopy of trees, then melt into the black sky, "these fellers've got ta think they're lucky ta be livin'…plain lucky, but they don't say it right out."

Cole and Shoemaker suddenly realized that a question lay beneath their friend's statement.

"Do ya thank God for bein' alive and forget it, or do ya sit down and try to figure out the workin's of it…give yerself a lesson?" Cole rasped, locking onto Jonah to challenge his hidden question.

"'Til the big fight comes, I guess I'll let Sergeant Vieland give the lessons," Jonah mumbled. The others, quietly contemplating the elusive strength they knew they would need in a major battle, accepted Jonah's naiveté, as they did their own.

The men's natural bent to disguise true feelings, a trait forged from unalloyed parental steel early in their rugged Midwestern lives, got in their way now. The possibility of sudden death loomed close, and as his companions deliberated in silence, Shoemaker got on his feet.

"I guess when the fightin' starts we just do what we know to do without thinkin', like we was trained to do...a little scared maybe, but no panic. Panic can get ya killed, I hear."

Cole, still gazing into the smoldering fire, blinking at its random flickers, looked at Shoemaker and cleared his throat, a prelude to a well-braised thought.

"I heard a Union general said once, 'Bein' scared is no part of a soldier's duty'. It was out West, I think."

"How can ya not be scared some?" Shoemaker shot back, looking steadily at Cole. But Cole simply nodded agreement.

Jonah rolled to his elbow. Both men looked at him. "Ya could get riled. I think anger takes over scared," Jonah mumbled, the idea taking shape as he spoke. "I think if yer spleen's up, ya don't worry about gettin' hurt," he added, his volume rising with his confidence. "Bein' angry could help ya do yer job and not get sidetracked, maybe killed. I think ya can get heated and still do the thing right, maybe even better...it might help ya stay on track."

Neither could think of an answer to the question lurking in their comrade's statement.

"I wonder how many of them got killed at Shiloh thought they wouldn't?" Shoemaker asked, his hypothetical drawing blank stares.

Jonah skirted the rhetorical challenge, a courtroom technique Shoemaker had apparently inherited from his father.

"The thing is," Jonah pushed, "how were the vet'rans who survived the fight thinkin' before it started? That's what I'd like ta find out, but they ain't talkin' much."

Cole managed a routine nod.

Shoemaker yawned, then Cole, but Jonah had not finished. "I think a little bile in the fight can't hurt, but I'm stickin' ta the trainin' we're gettin' from the old war horses as the main thing. We got plenty'a practiced men know how ta stay alive, even if they don't say much. God gives us the direction, the army gives us the tools, the vet'rans show us how ta use 'em. That's the way I look at it, anyhow."

The men backed off and spread their bedrolls, each diverting to pleasant thoughts, clearing the path for mind-cleansing sleep. Jonah, however, lay captured by the conversation for more than an hour, searching for clues that might lead a young man to self-reliance in battle.

. . . . .

At 10 o'clock on Wednesday, the 21st of May, the regiment, busy since sunup cutting down trees for a corduroy road, suddenly heard the throaty thud of cannon close on their right. The concussion swept over the axe-wielding men, stunning several mid-stroke, freezing them in the confusion of the moment, their bare backs glistening in the warm sun. A pounding fusillade erupted in the distance and the long drum roll racked the air, riddled by yet more staccato blasts of cannon. As if on signal, the men swept across the meadow separating them from their weapons, their glazed torsos and polished axe blades glinting as they surged into the trees, snowflakes swirling in a wind gust.

The soldiers struggled into their shirts, their silvery backsides warping into a dark thundercloud as they dove for cover behind log earthworks fronting the meadow.

Nearly breathless, the men fumbled up their muskets and trappings, the clatter pierced now and then by the bark of company sergeants.

Leaping over the redoubt and into the trees with the rest, Jonah snatched up his rifle and belted ammunition box, throwing himself into position behind the log revetment running just inside the trees skirting the meadow. He rolled to his back, loaded, tamped and spun to his stomach, slapping the musket's stock against his cheek.

Through a devised gap in the earthworked logs he saw shadows, glints and flickers moving in the woods beyond the meadow, only fifty yards from the copse where they had been cutting. At that moment he knew the big fight had found him. The underbrush began to crackle as Federal infantry broke through the woods to the rear of the line. The advancing infantry split left and right as they cleared the heavy timber, racing for position on the flanks of the fortified battle line, and then they began to dig in, flinging dirt like burrowing badgers.

Jonah glanced back to see Captain Meredith skillfully weaving his black stallion back and forth behind the prone soldiers of Company C. The captain shouted no orders. The horse's syncopated hoof-frump suddenly ended with a piercing whinny and a wet snort.

The Federal line fell to a vibrant quiet; the men searched the trees beyond the meadow, glimpsing drifting shadows. To his left and right Jonah heard the metallic "schlick" of ramrods springing from gun barrels, mingled with the muffled grunts of the reinforcements rolling to their stomachs. A quarter-mile of men now lay in position, elbow-to-elbow, ready to fire. No order came. The woods opposite had stopped moving.

Four teams of horses, each team trailing an artillery limber and cannon, came crashing through the undergrowth behind the waiting soldiers, threading their way up the tangled cut made by the reinforcements. As the horses cleared the timber, a young artillery major with a thin blond beard danced his frothing, black-speckled roan alongside each driver, pointing his sword toward unobstructed positions behind the entrenchments. The guns lunged forward, the major shouting *"Shell shot! Case shot at the ready!"* after them. The artillerymen unhitched the snorting teams while still on the run, snatching out tongue pins and spinning the cannon around and rolling in their limbers by hand. Above the jangling rumble, Jonah heard battery officers shouting orders to their gun crews. The teamsters quickly led their animals back into the woods; all fell silent once again. The major swept off his black, broad-brimmed hat, slapped his roan's lathered flank and galloped to an open hillock on the right.

Jonah gazed across the field, unaware that his senses had honed to razor sharpness. Each second seemed like minutes. Waiting became death delivered. His mind raced, struggling to deal with imagined happenings. His Minié box suddenly felt empty. He reached back, fumbled its heft and knew it was too soon. No longer able to grasp the tempo of time, he now found himself drifting, disconnected from his body. With superhuman concentration, he fought to synchronize his brain with the reality of time and place.

He glanced left and right, saw Sergeant Vieland, Elias Cole and Sam Fry, but when he looked away he could not be certain how long ago he had seen them. He looked again. Resting his forehead on his musket stock, Jonah shut his eyes and struggled to recapture the pace of reality, but his mental warp would not lock into the muffled knock and swell surrounding him. He could not remember how long ago the artillery had arrived. Panic began to puncture his distorted sense of reality.

He tried to think himself through the reloading process but could not stay with it to the end. A debilitating force, intense and overpowering, had seized his mind, and he could no longer control his thoughts. Lost and alone, Jonah longed for God's calming grace that would not come. *Now!* he prayed, happen *now!* Something happen *now!*

He heard a faint rip on the far right across the meadow, the slow tearing of butcher paper gradually growing louder as it swept left into the freshly leafed-out trees swimming in the sunlight opposite. A white plume of smoke seemed to give birth to the ripping rattle, an artist's practiced brush stroke, a milky pedestal underpinning the dark forest marble.

The ripping sound, at first a staccato whisper, rose to a whirring crack as it surged along the tree line across the meadow. Just as it reached the trees opposite him, a swarm of screaming shot tore through the branches above his head, showering him with leaves and twigs. Jonah reached back and clutched his cartridge box. Still too soon.

Suddenly a thousand Confederates wearing a discordant array of gray, butternut and motley, emerged in a wavy line from the far trees, as if it were an accidental stumbling forward. Here and there an enemy kneeled and fired, but most came slowly over the meadow, their weapons clutched against their fronts or sides. Jonah reached back and felt his canteen. Not now.

He concentrated on the advancing enemy, focused on a tall, bearded man wearing a gray slouch hat, high-stepping straight ahead. Then the entire enemy phalanx began to dash forward, their bayonets flashing in the sunlight, charging the waiting Yankees, their piercing wail cleaving the air. The Rebels' howl clicked Jonah's mental clock into gear, aligning time. He knew it was now, knew for certain what was unfolding before him, and knew what to do about it. His anger surged. Here come the bastards...an abomination on the Nation's ass...lice in the hair of the Virgin...they.... His sweaty cheek smacked his musket stock. Close, thirty rods, too close.

Captain Meredith's deep roar rippled down the line: *Low! Low! Aim low!...Fire!* Jonah squeezed and rolled, instantly deaf. Anger still stabbed through him and he focused on his action with blind determination. Cartridge–ball–ram–cap–roll. *Fire!* Before he could twist to his back to load again, a hot blast seared his nape, blowing his forage cap against the log in front. A stinging cloud of dirt and twigs slammed the back of his head. He glanced around to see a six-pounder rolling into battery behind him, unelevated, repositioning to spew canister over his head. Smoldering cannon wadding torched off fires in the leaves along the revetment. Men swatted the flames with their forage caps.

Jonah loaded and rolled, swept his ten-pound Springfield onto the log in front, slammed its butt to his shoulder as if it were weightless. The shooting stopped. He saw only Southern backsides going south. The mottled line of retreating Rebels faded into the dark woods, a few stragglers helping wounded comrades escape the open meadow. Twisted bodies sprinkled the ground in front of Jonah, some splayed on their backs, gazing skyward, sightless. The tall bearded Rebel lay among them.

He rolled to his side, hesitated, and then ran his rammer down his weapon's barrel, uncertain if he had fired the last load. A spike of fear shot through him. The rod measured one unfired ball. He had not panicked, had not double-loaded. He watched others checking their weapons for load. Close on his right he heard Sergeant Vieland's calm, distinctive clack.

"They ain't gonna be gettin' it done that'a way. They won't be scatterin' buffaloes that'a way."

Another voice came from the left, charged with excitement: "*Damn!* We sent 'em *skeedaddlin'!*"

Cheers rose in a ground swell of emotion, the impulsive huzzah seeming to sweep away the gray smoke layered in the trees overhead. Men sprang to their feet waving their caps, their powder-darkened lips matching their sweat-drenched uniforms.

"Down, *down! Dammit, down!*" the company sergeants barked, shattering the men's spontaneous elation with lightning bolt commands.

The men jumped back to cover. Once again charged clouds of silence swept over them. They lay until nightfall, when the company sergeants ordered out their recruits to bring in the enemy dead. Before picking him up, Jonah gently closed the eyes of the tall bearded man. As he did his anger dissolved, leaving confusion in its wake.

Word came down the line that the scouts reported the Rebels had moved south. Further attack was highly unlikely. The Federals collected their equipment, fell into ranks and marched back to camp.

Casualties were light for the 26th Ohio: One man killed in Company K. But the 32nd Indiana reported four killed.

The long drum roll sounded again at 1 a.m., and the men quicktimed in the dark, back to the battle line fronting the meadow. They spent the rest of the night lying quietly alert behind the log revetment. Nothing happened.

. . . . .

At 6 a.m. on Friday, May 30, as C Company finished its hardtack and ham breakfast, a thunderous explosion to the south, toward Corinth, brought everyone to his feet, most with gaping mouths.

"That's gotta be the dee-struction of Beauregard's magazine, so's General Halleck can't get his hands on it," Private Shoemaker announced, seeming to take credit for the blast. "Dynee-mightee!"

Jonah watched a huge column of black smoke climb into the sky, bloom and drift eastward, spreading itself across the heavens. The fume dissolved to a thin gray blanket covering the morning sun, giving the eastern horizon a lurid glow. The stunning detonation raised the soldiers' spirits, giving the weary men visible hope for success in their seemingly endless struggle to capture Corinth. Company C remained bivouacked all day, watching columns of lighthearted troops march past.

At 9 a.m. the next morning, the 26th Ohio Volunteer Infantrymen broke camp, loaded their tents and equipment into wagons and fell into ranks. At 11 a.m. they stacked arms in a churchyard on the outskirts of Corinth, Mississippi, surrounded by 100,000 friendly Federal troops.

Jonah thought he might be a veteran now, but was not quite sure. He helped round up the 2,000 prisoners taken on the assault, mostly sick and wounded. Then, with inspired determination, Jonah guarded the apprehended Rebels and his captured manhood carefully.

. . . . .

Relevant Diary Entries

Sat May 3rd
Reveille at 3 A.M. and started on the march at 5 A.M. went 4 miles and encamped our wagons came up at 3 P.M. we heard sharp skirmishing with canon and musketry at 4 P.M. we formed a line of battle by order of Col Fyffe broke ranks at 5 P.M. with orders to lay on our arms.

Sunday May 4th 1862
We formed a line of battle at day-light we broke ranks with orders to march at a moments notice. I attended church in the 17th Ind and 26th Ohio Regts in the A.M. Rained all the forenoon and night.

Sat May the 10th

I was detailed for Regimental guard. We had orders to march at 10 A.M. We struck tents and fell in ranks and marched at 1 P.M. We went 5 miles we crossed the Ten & Miss line at 2 P.M. The Regt laid on their arms Co C went on picket

Sunday May 11th

I was relieved from guard at 9 A.M. I went to church in the 17th Ind There was a minister preached from Terre Haut Ind. He spoke in our Regt in the P.M. While he was speaking we received orders to march We fell in and marched ½ mile and encamped and pitched our tents Our Co came in at 5 P.M. and while eating supper the Regt was ordered on picket we went out at dark and laid on our arms all night. We were called up once by picket firing in our advance. The 26th signed the Pay Rolls this A.M.

Mond May 12th 1862

We formed a line of battle at 3 ½ A.M. and remained until daylight when we rested in line. The division formed a line of battle at 10 A.M. and returned to camp at noon. Our Regt were relieved from picket at 2 P.M. We were called out at 3 oclock to draw our pay. We marched to headquarters and got our pay and came to camp at 4 P.M.

Sat May 17th

Struck tents at 6 A.M. We fell in ranks and remained there until 1 P.M. and we had to pitch tents again we staid in camp until 4 p.m. when we were ordered to fall in ranks we were off in a few minutes and marched about four miles to our front about ½ mile from the rebel pickets we halted at 8 oclock and layed by our arms in the bushes. We were called up several times during the night by frequent firing of the pickets

Sun May 18th 62
Skirmishing commenced at daylight between the rebel and our pickets which was kept up all day. The rebels fired a few shots with artillery but did no harm.

Mond May 19th
The pickets commenced firing again at daylight We marched at 11 A.M. back about one mile and the Regt was sent on picket There was four Companies sent out as skirmishers the line was about 26 rods in our advance. They were firing all the P.M. The rebels opened a battery of artillery on us at 4 P.M. but was soon satisfied by a couple of our batteries giving them a few shell rather fromisquously. Rainy night our tents were moved up to us this A.M.

Wed May 21st
Our Regt was detailed for fatigue in the morning we went in front of our fortifications and were chopping trees until 10 A.M. when heavy cannonading was heard on our right but a short distance from us we fell back into the intrenchments there was sharp skirmishing along the lines all day. We had several wounded but the rebels were repulsed.

Thurs May 22nd
The enemy attacked our pickets in the night and we were called into the intrenchments at 1 A.M. and layed on our arms until daylight We remained there until 5 P.M. and again came into camp There is heavy cannonading again this evening. We laid in the intrench again all night.

Tues May 27th
We went out on picket at 8 A.M. There was skirmishing all day. One man of Co K was killed and two or three wounded of the 32 Ind.

Wed May 28th
We came into camp at 8 A.M. We were called into the intrenchments at noon There was heavy firing in General Pope and Nelsons and McCooks brigades all day with heavy musketry There was two batteries and 160 prisoners taken by our side

Friday May 30
There was a heavy explosion heard at 6 A.M. in the direction of Corinth followed by heavy columns of smoke supposed to be the explosion of the rebel magazine (which was afterwards found to be so) We marched into the intrenchments at 7 A.M. and returned to camp at 10 A.M. Troops are passing all day but don't know their destination

Sat May 31st
We fell in ranks at 9 A.M. and marched into Corinth where we arrived at 10 A.M. We stacked arms and remained there the rest of the day.

4.

"And the soldiers likewise demanded of him, saying, And what shall we do? And he said unto them, Do violence to no man...and be content with your wages." Luke 3:14

On the march east from Corinth, Jonah simply said, "We ain't done a lick a good since we conquered Corinth," and his audience attacked him like wasps defending their larvae.

John Shoemaker was the first to sting. "We tore up them railroad tracks they was usin', Jonah...an' kept the grit-grinders on the run pretty good, don't ya know."

Having finished their warmed ham and lima bean suppers, Sam Fry and Elias Cole stepped in for the kill. "We done our part, stoppin' enemy reinforcements from gettin' to Beatty's Third when they was rippin' up the rails, too, Jonah," Fry asserted, watching Jonah scrape ham grease from his tin plate with half a hardtack biscuit, and then added, "an' after the Rebs fixed 'em again, we rips 'em again, an' that ain't a bad summer's work."

"The Charleston rails won't do the Secesh no good now, thanks to us," Cole announced in a rare confirmation, his eyes following Jonah as he rose to his feet.

"Sergeant Vieland says we're headed north to Meridianville tomorrow, and the rails keep goin' east from here, so ain't the Rebs comin' outta Georgia still supplied against us?" Jonah asked. "The long and the short of it is we worked all summer fer nothin'. When we gonna get a chance to teach the Rebs another lesson, like we did at Corinth?"

Sam Fry sensed a hollow ring in Jonah's words. "Look, Jonah, we marched all the way from Iuka to the cane brake and we're still breathin'. What's wrong with that?" he asked, smiling.

"George ain't breathin'," Cole mumbled.

George Beasley had died at Hamburg Landing, Alabama, from a wound, according to Doctor Sabine, gotten in the attack in the meadow on the crawl to Corinth. A ball had sliced open Beasley's forehead; it healed quickly but he had trouble understanding simple ideas after that, and his speech never returned to normal. His tongue kept hitting the roof of his mouth, making him spit words as if they were stuck in his throat.

"Brain cyclone did it...that don't count," Fry pronounced, staring at the ground.

Shoemaker ended the discussion: "Well, we'll say goodbye to Moresville tomorrow, the best river fishin' there ever was, and blackberry pickin' like I never seen before," he said, rising. They went to their bedrolls.

The men had been on full dress review, marching and standing in the sun all afternoon for General Wood, the division commander. Then they had formed once more before supper to witness an official cannon salute to the Nation's birth. It was the Fourth of July, 1862. They were sunburned and exhausted.

Although the Corinth campaign had given Jonah new confidence, as well as veteran status, he felt cheated by the army's fruitless march through Northern Alabama. Unlike Corinth, there was no clearly defined enemy line, and the Federal generals seemed unable to find one. Eager for action that would end the war, he had begun to experience a new frustration.

His malaise had begun on June 15 at Florence, Alabama, where the regiment was ordered to tear down a railroad station instead of tearing into the enemy. The result of their tearing turned out to be as devastating as a battle, even worse, since the Rebels had nothing to do with it. Jonah remembered having attended church that morning, and when the preacher raised his hands during the benediction he looked straight at Jonah and seemed to bless him. Jonah credited his escape from the depot calamity to the blessing experience.

About forty men, roughly half the company, had been detailed to tear the roof from the Florence railroad station. It was almost sundown and they had nearly finished, so they were working hard to get the job done before dark. Suddenly the whole building began to sway, and within seconds the peak collapsed and walls caved in. It hurt fifteen men severely, a few of which were collecting torn-off shingles that had fallen inside the building. Standing on a hip rafter drinking water from a ladle, Jonah beat the tin scoop he held in his hand to the ground.

The last thing he remembered was watching a dozen boys ripping the final shingles from an eave with spades. A few lucky tumblers scattered like ants when they hit the ground, having somehow avoided serious injury, but most of the roof crew lay where they landed. For them, the sun had set with a crimson flash.

Although trapped under splintered rafters and planks, Jonah could still be seen by his rescuers–his left boot protruded from the pile. The first thing he heard were John Shoemaker, Elias Cole and Sam Fry calling his name, flinging boards from the pile like crazed prospectors chasing a vein of California gold. They pulled him out, carried him off to the infirmary tent and visited him every day until he became well enough to walk without help. It took nearly a week to recover. On the sixth day the lightning bolts finally stopped shooting down his back every time he took a step.

Fry was the first man to jump to Jonah's rescue, his wide eyes glistening like two greased eggs sizzling in a skillet. A feisty rascal of slight build, he rarely showed emotion and often outlasted bigger men at physical work, but that time he was obviously excited.

For those few men who got to know Sam Fry well, he proved to be a pleasant natured optimist with a nice sense of humor, but his hefty mustache looked threatening and could "blink the devil," according to Shoemaker. His friends believed that Sam kept his lip hair waxed in a circle at the ends just to see how his looks affected others. He rarely scowled, but when he did his face became a tornado twisting in for the kill, and no stranger messed with him then, not even men half again larger.

While confined to the infirmary, Jonah had time to think about his close friends, Cole, Fry and Shoemaker, God-fearing men who did no illegal card gambling and never stole corn whiskey from farmers' barns like so many did. Their closeness, he concluded, centered on Christian self-discipline, which they all recognized in each other, a virtue, according to Reverend Sable, that can pull a man through any adversity. So, if we can endure these kinds of hardships, Jonah reasoned, why not confront the enemy instead of just destroying his train depots?

After the Florence incident, Jonah compulsively focused on the army's refusal to send the 26th after the Rebels; his inexplicable waves of discontent began to intensify. The reason that they did not push south and confront the enemy, he concluded, was the regiment's "new" weapons.

General Halleck had decided that each regiment should carry the same caliber muskets, so the hardtack hawkers, the quartermasters, could get ammunition to the men more efficiently. But Jonah could not recall having trouble finding balls for his .58 caliber on the Corinth attack.

During *Shiloh Church* and the Corinth Campaign, Jonah carried a Model 1855 Springfield rifle-musket with a flat bayonet knife that had a comfortable grip. Butchering a land shark (a hog living in Tennessee) took only five minutes with the knife, and it was excellent for throwing, as he had often demonstrated. But then the 26th was issued Model 1842 muskets that had what looked like a potato-skewer spike for a bayonet, and no rear sight. It shot .69 caliber balls, and a full cartridge pouch, the men quickly realized, could send less determined soldiers to their knees after an hour of quicktime. Measuring two inches longer than the 1855, the replacement muskets required an ape with a four foot arm to load, Shoemaker had pointed out while watching Fry struggle with his. The guns were not as accurate, having no rifling in the barrel, which made Elias Cole particularly angry. But the exchange of weapons did not seem to upset Sergeant Vieland.

"Which Reb's more dead?" he asked, overhearing a complaint during breakfast at Red Rock Junction, "one with a .58 caliber hole or a .69 caliber hole?"

When the regiment marched into Decatur, Alabama, on June 30 without enemy contact, Jonah had reached his limit. After supper he took an empty place over the latrine trench between Shotwell and Sergeant Vieland.

"I heard these oldfangled muskets'll keep us out of the fight 'till worms bark and skunks smell sweet," he said to Shotwell. They squatted in silence, knowing Vieland had heard the comment. Finally the sergeant rose and hitched up his trousers.

"These here '42 muskets are jest as good as any," he

grunted, almost cracking a smile. "If ya don't know how
ta handle 'em proper, I'll show ya...quit yer bellyachin'."
Vieland's authority slammed into Jonah, rocking him
backward. He nearly fell into the slit trench.

What would Reverend Sable say to Vieland? If any
man understood the black and white of the Great Crusade
against the South, the reverend did, a logical man who
could grasp the facts of any important issue. Would he
try to explain to Vieland that a fruitless stroll through the
Alabama countryside is not a part of God's plan for the
Nation?

Jonah's frustration temporarily lost its edge when he
and his comrades were able to go fishing on the Tennessee
River for a few days. The men had appropriated a fishing
skiff they discovered when scouting Jackson Island for
signs of the enemy, calling it war booty. Testing the river's
backwaters and eddies with worm and jerky-baited hooks,
they finally found a good catfish hole. Shoemaker caught
a thirty-pounder and suddenly became an expert angler,
describing how the drift-down factor is related to current
velocity and sinker heft.

Chaplain Vessey, Sergeant Major Hawkins, and Sam
Hutchison from Company I went with them the next day,
everyone taking turns rowing without regard to rank. They
landed twelve "pole snappers," which drew Doctor Sabine
and Colonel Boring to the water the following afternoon,
Private Shoemaker serving as their fishing guide. Jonah
went along, expecting to hear a few words about the conduct
of the war, but the officers simply enjoyed themselves,
comparing fish fry recipes and reminiscing about boyhood
outings.

On the third and final day they fished, the steamer
Lady Pike churned past close aboard to starboard. "Thar
ain't no females on deck...," Sam Fry remarked as the ship
approached, then added, "...it's haulin' troops, look at them

recruits idlin' at the rail in thar new uniforms. Look, them uniforms still got thar bundle wrinkles." The rest of the party, Jonah, Elias and John, glanced at each other and smiled. Content with his faded clothing, a sign of a veteran, Jonah's smile lingered.

A week after the four fishermen entertained the regiment with their war-booty boat, Sergeant Vieland called the company into ranks and presented Jonah with corporal chevrons. From then on, the sergeant kept Jonah busy with official duties—ensuring that each man had sufficient rations and water for the march, inventorying supplies and mustering men for work detail. When on the move, Jonah often led foraging parties. Although Jonah's duties allowed little time to worry about the war's progress at first, his efficiency quickly improved, permitting time for anxiety.

. . . . .

The regiment turned north from Moresville, Alabama, moving quickly through Huntsville and Meridianville, then into Tennessee. The 26th camped on the Elk River at Fayetteville, Tennessee, on the fifteenth of July, 1862, and two days later moved to Shelbyville, then across to Winchester and back to Fayetteville. At sundown on the Nineteenth, north of Tullahoma, they ran into General Negley's division and camped overnight next to the 78th Pennsylvania. Jonah discovered that Negley had his boys marching in circles just as the 26th was, and with as little enemy contact.

Except for one prisoner, a lost Secesh messenger, taken on Friday August 8, the 26th did not see a Rebel until Wednesday August 13, when they were attacked at the Eight Mile Woods south of Sam Springs. The Confederate brigade lay in a dense stand of trees along a creek bed, which ran alongside the road into Sam Springs. The Federals, warned just in time, threw themselves into a ditch on the opposite side of the road just as the Rebels' first volley barked over their heads with demoralizing fury. But the Rebels turned and ran immediately, disappearing before a counterattack could be mounted. The Federals suffered no casualties, other than a broken leg when a man from Company B jumped down onto a rock.

"We kicked them road apples off the pike," Jonah reflected as the regiment reformed. Cole, a seeker of truth, could not let the comment pass.

"Naw...not this time, Jonah. This is a feint an' a thrust... that was the feint part, the thrust comes next."

"You sure?" Shoemaker mumbled.

"Nope, I ain't. But maybe we'll find out shortly. The thing smells like a plan, the way they took off."

"Too damn hot to play hide an' seek," Fry said as the company moved out at rout step.

But the warm August days began to cool at Sam Springs. On picket duty the next evening, half the men chose to lay in the fading sunshine rather than seek shade. They were deployed along the eastern edge of a wooded hillock, staring into a meadow of trampled grass where the enemy had camped only two days before. Even though the Rebels had left the area, Jonah did not sleep that night, listening for sounds in the darkness in front of him.

Just south of Mill Springs, Company C went "nigger hunting" with Company H; their "rummage in the woodpile" turned up eighty-two blacks. By the time the 26th arrived in Camp Verville at the end of August, they had captured, in addition to the blacks, two Rebel prisoners, seven horses, four mules, seventeen pounds of flour and three Secesh tents. The "coloreds" were employed on work details for pay, mostly cutting and clearing, but a few were kept by the officers for staff chores.

On Wednesday, August 27, the regiment, now a part of Wood's Division, marched northeast at sunrise, bivouacking two miles west of McMinnville the same evening. Miserable rain showers pelted the men for the next four days. During a break in a heavy rain on Saturday morning, Company C was ordered to police the regimental ground, even though it still drizzled. Just as they finished throwing their trash into a wagon, the long roll beat the regiment to arms. Corporal Hommen led the company in its mad scramble to form ranks. The men fell into a line of battle and quickly swept east, but could not find the enemy, so returned to camp. After the noon meal, Sergeant Vieland once again warned them to be ready on a moment's notice.

Heavy cannonading began to thunder to the east that afternoon. The regiment finally marched out in columns at four o'clock, quicktimed northwest on the Nashville Road for eight miles, and then doublequicked for two more miles.

From the doublequick, the men rolled into a line of battle, dashing to overtake Secesh cavalry walking their mounts in the drizzle, not expecting infantry because of the rain. The 26th came at the cavalry from downwind; without seeing the enemy the Federals sensed what lay ahead.

"I smell horseshit an' wet saddle leather!" Fry boomed as they loped over the top of a wooded knoll.

"Smell it? I can hear the critters chompin' thar bits!" Shoemaker wheezed.

The company cleared the trees just in time to see the south end of General Forrest's horses galloping north, all 1500 of them, disappearing into the woods beyond a range of cleared farmland. As they swept down the hillock, Sergeant Vieland ordered his men to hit the mud and fire from the prone position for accuracy, and they were able to get off one or two shots each before the routed enemy escaped. Jonah had fired twice and reloaded again before the "cease fire" bugle sounded. Woods division, the 26th in the lead, followed the scattered cavalry until dark, and then turned back.

"We could'a picked off them horses' asses like chickens in a coop if they hadn't a run, ain't that so?" Shoemaker growled, glancing at Jonah as the regiment formed along the Nashville road.

"Maybe," Jonah answered, cradling his musket. "We had the range on 'em. I guess these here arm busters'll do in a pinch."

It had stopped raining. The air carried a fresh fragrance and the march back became almost a pleasant evening stroll. Jonah recounted their return to camp in a letter to his mother:

"Everyone's spirits still boiled from the chase, but we calmed ourselves by singing "Mister Here's Your Mule" and "Rallied Round the Flag." Then about halfway back we got surprised by a sight, and it locked up our jaws. The sky cleared, letting the moon shine down white and strong, almost like day, and the wet fields mirroring the moonlight, and the trees shining like silver. Our regiment came up on the crest of a hill and we could see the main force just ahead come to a willow grove, maybe a dozen trees or so, sparkling like winter ice in the moonlight. All a sudden light burst up from the trees, their branches somehow taking to flight.

"It finally dawned on me it was a flock of roosted birds lifting off all at once, having been scared to flight. They shot straight out at Purdy's Gap, black as pitch, swooping and turning then disappearing. Then a thousand silver dots, like a school of scared minnows dived back on us in the moonlight. They covered the whole sky over our heads, and the boys started gettin excited, hootin and yellin. Then, sweeping up for another attack they boiled black, disappearing in the sky again. But we could judge where they was after they climbed, cause when they reached their height they turned into a big gray cloud, then swooped back down, flashing silver again. Them birds kept it up until the whole column passed, then I dont know what they did. Went to roost again, maybe.

"They had to be black, but black birds dont change color as far as I know, turn white all a sudden, and that puzzled me at first. When they climbed they stayed black, hid by the sky, and thats when I got muddled, thinkin some different birds came at us when they turned silver. The moonlight did it, but it was hard to believe at the time."

The next day the 58th Indiana went back to the site of the cavalry rout and scouted the grounds, capturing four wounded Rebels and six horses, one farrier's wagon, and a hog trough full of guns. Jonah went to the 58th that evening to inspect five Adams .44s and two pistol carbines they had captured, weapons he had never seen before.

He lay on his new rubber blanket that night listening to men murmur and crickets chirp, trying to make sense of the Rebel rout. Forrest's horsemen had scattered like ants, but he had not heard a Secesh bugle give the order to retreat. Were they panicked? If his friends ever ran away without the withdraw order, would he run with them? Would he ever…run to save his life?

. . . . .

Relevant Diary Entries

Mond June 9th
We resumed our march at 5 A.M. and encamped at Tuscumbia Springs, Ala, at 5 P.M.

Wed June 11th 62
I and Olmsted and 4 of Co I boys went up to the foot of Muscle shoals. And landed on Jacksons Island and captured

a skiff

Thurs June 12ᵗʰ 1862
I help ferry the Col and Co A across the river. We received orders to march to Tuscumbia landing We packed up and started at 1 P.M. The Chaplain Sergt Major two from Co I and myself went down the river in a skiff

Friday June 13ᵗʰ 1862
We policed the parade ground in the morning The steamer Lady Pike came up A.M. and left at 1 P.M. I went fishing with Dr Sabine Col Boring in a boat in the P.M.

Sunday June 15ᵗʰ
It was a very warm day a part of Buels came to Florence today. Our Co was detailed to cross the river and tear down an old R.R. building. About 40 of us were on roof tearing off the shingles when the walls gave away and the whole pile of us fell with the roof to the ground. It hurt 15 of us pretty severely I among the number. We were carried to the boat and taken to camp about midnite.

Wed June 25
All quiet in camp George Bensley died at Hamburg landing this p.m.

Fri July 4ᵗʰ 1862
Our brigade had general review by Gen Wood. There was a national salute fired at sundown

Thurs July 10ᵗʰ
Had drill in the A.M. and J. B. Richardson and I went blackberring there was a heavy rain while we was out

Mond July 14ᵗʰ 1862

We marched at 4 A.M. and arrived at Huntsville at 11
A.M. We marched again at 4 P.M. We passed through
Meredienville at 7 P.M. and encamped at 10

Sun July 20ᵗʰ
We marched again at 5 A.M. We encamped at noon at
Winchester springs; This place was a great summer
resterance

Thurs July 24ᵗʰ
Sam Fry and I went and got some apples, butter and
chickens. I attended prayer meeting in the evening.

Sun July 27ᵗʰ
We had church at 10 A.M. S. G. Fry, T. G. Gow, G. Gibson
and I went out foreging in the P.M. Prayer meeting in the
evening

Friday Aug 8ᵗʰ 1862
Cos C. and H went out to hunt niggers. We brought in
eight niggers and one prisoner

Sat Aug 30ᵗʰ
The Regt was poliecing the Regimental ground when the
long roll beat and we fell in line of battle and marched
out We soon came in with orders to be ready to fall in
at a moments warning. There was cannonading East of us
all day. Our brigade, with the exceptions of one Regt had
orders to march at 3 ½ P.M. We started at 4 and went on
quicktime out on the Nashville road, 8 miles and then went
on double quick 2 miles and overtook Gen Forests cavalry
1500 of them. We opened one battery of artillery on them,
and the 26ᵗʰ Regt formed a line of battle and marched on
them. They wouldn't stand a fight but broke into regular
skedadling rout every man for himself. We followed them

until dark and then marched back for camp, where we arrived at 11 oclock. There was one wagon, several revolvers, and guns captured. There was supposed to be several killed. We found several dead horses. There was no harm done on our side.

Sun Aug 31ˢᵗ
We mustered for pay in the P.M. The 58 Ind Regt went out where we had the fight and found 4 wounded secesh, captured several horses, and quite a number of revolvers and guns. There was church in the evening.

. . . . .

Colonel E. P. Fyffe's Report on the Rout of General Forrest at McMinnville

(Official Record, Vol XVI, Series 1, Part 2)

HEADQUARTERS FIFTEENTH BRIGADE,
Near McMinnville, Ten., August 31, 1862

SIR: In pursuance to orders from Brigadier-General Wood to cut off General Forrest and his command, who was passing to the westward and within 2 miles of this camp, making his way northward, and upon five minutes' notice, after procuring a guide, I marched in a circuitous route through the woods to the Murfreesborough and McMinnville road, a distance of 6 miles from camp. I pushed forward in the direction of Murfreesborough in quick-time until I came to an open country, where at some distance across the fields I discovered the column of General Forrest, consisting entirely of cavalry.

The enemy having become aware of my presence at this time

there commenced an exciting race between his command
of cavalry and my column of infantry for the intersection
of the two roads. I ordered my command forward at a
double-quick, which they obeyed cheerfully, although they
had marched several miles at quick-time without water. I
discovered when about 400 or 500 yards distant from the
junction of the roads that General Forrest had formed his
command in line of battle to receive my attack....

...After firing a few rounds the enemy's lines gave way in
the center. His right wing (the Texan Rangers and some
Alabama troops) were forced to take the back track to our
left, while General Forrest, with his left wing, scampered
off in the direction of Murfreesborough....

...In a very short time the enemy were entirely dispersed in
every direction; so much so that it was with great difficulty I
could determine on which road it would be most profitable
to pursue him. I immediately concluded to follow him on
the Murfreesborough road, but it had grown so dark that
I was enabled to pursue him but about 2 miles, when I
was forced to abandon the chase in consequence of the
men and animals suffering for water. I returned to camp
the same night, arriving about 11 o'clock. The ground over
which we fought presented every indication of the utmost
confusion and consternation on the part of the enemy, the
woods and roads being strewn with arms, wearing apparel,
&c. Accompanying this I have the honor to present a list
of the property that fell into our hands. The actual loss
of the enemy I had no means of ascertaining, but from
the statements of citizens subsequently received and from
his own admissions his loss must have been from 18 to 20
killed and wounded....

I have the honor to be, very respectfully, your obedient

servant,
E. P. FYFFE
Colonel Twenty-sixth Ohio Volunteers, Commanding.

5.

"For we know in part, and we prophesy in part. But when that which is perfect is come, then that which is in part shall be done away." 1 Corinthians 13:9,10

The soldier's rain-soaked shirts threw off wisps of steam as they pitched their tents in a soggy pasture just two miles north of Shelbyville, Kentucky, at 1:30 p.m. on Thursday, the seventeenth of July. A hurry-up sounding reveille had erupted at 4 a.m.; the regiment moved out without filling in latrines or eating. As they marched, cool air had blown in from the west, bringing with it torturous rain squalls. It was the last leg of a two-day trek from the Elk River to Shelbyville, most of it made at a near run, which had the effect of heating the men until their clothing seemed to smoke in the chilly air. They finally ate breakfast at three p.m. in the center of the soggy cow pasture.

After wolfing down salt pork, tepid pea soup and a ladle of thin coffee, Company C helped dig latrines and timber-in walking paths until the light began to fade, then inhaled a late supper. Captain Meredith ordered his soldiers out on picket duty to replace the unfed men of Company A—again his company would not get a full night's sleep.

At sunrise the following morning, before the pickets were relieved by Company B, a local Arabian horse breeder, Mr. Reed, invited Sam Fry, Elias Cole, John Shoemaker, and Jonah to his farm for breakfast. The Reed place lay just a ten-minute walk south of their picket line.

"What horse farm?" Sergeant Vieland rumbled when Jonah asked permission to mess at the Reeds, "I don't smell nothin'."

"Maybe the cavalry bought his horses, Sergeant."

"More likely Morgan stole 'em. Be back for morning colors, Corporal Hommen. And, ah, bring fresh vegetables if they got extra."

The four men sat on a stack of split-oak cordwood ten feet from the back door of the Reed house, waiting, their knapsacks at their feet. The majestic, two-story farmhouse loomed above them, its split-cedar shingles aglow in the early morning sunshine. Mrs. Reed finally came through the kitchen doorway carrying china plates and silverware, delivered them to the men's laps, and then rushed back inside. She reappeared balancing heaped platters in each hand, from which she spooned hot scrambled eggs, ham, slices of corn bread and thick molasses onto her precious dishes resting on the soldiers' knees. Everyone thanked her; Sam Fry complimented her on the china plates and polished silverware. They ate in silence.

The food disappeared quickly, once again bringing to light the china plates' delicate silver tracings of artful equestrian scenes. The sketches reminded Jonah of the annual horse show at the Delaware County Fair that he had always looked forward to as a boy. Relaxed family meals, laced with casual conversation and eaten from porcelain plates, he realized, were far away now. He glanced at his silent comrades, knowing that the civilian dinnerware and home-cooked meal had also brought them thoughts of the past.

He rested his plate on his haversack, fingered up his tin cup from a snap hook on his belt, rose to his feet and idled down a rocked pathway toward the covered well. He paused to gaze across the feed-yard to the hip-roofed barn, then past it to the damp trees, their glistening leaves thrust into the cloudless morning sky as they struggled for life—giving light. The barn's central aisle led straight through the structure to reveal the thick woods beyond. Jonah could see patches of bright berries riding waist high amid barbed thickets, forming nature's picket line, protecting the silent society of wet tree trunks behind them.

A fleeting motion in the barn caught his eye, a movement in the shadows midway along the railed pens serving as weather stables for expensive horses. Suddenly a young woman appeared in the corridor carrying two staved buckets partially hidden in the folds of her white skirts. She seemed not to notice him as she turned and slowly walked into the darkness on her right. Jonah's eyes narrowed, straining against the backlight as he searched the barn's murky bowels. Was she actually there? Then she came to the aisle again and paused. Her clean, innocent perfection stunned him, locking his mind to a standstill in mid-stroke, suspending time, sweeping away all else.

She floated away down the barn's dim passage and swept into the sunlight beyond. Her thick, black hair, drawn into a tight bun at her nape, glistened in the sudden flood of light. Framed by the barn's symmetrical doorways, she paused in the sunlight, her flowing white skirts rippling in a soft wind swirl, startling Jonah with their brilliance. She suddenly swung to the right and disappeared.

Jonah glanced back at the sated soldiers behind him, listening to their witticisms as they anticipated the day's unfolding and tomorrow's weather. They could not have seen the girl. He fought an impulse to run after her, watch her without being seen. He turned away feeling an eerie emptiness creep over him, the strange emotion bringing with it an unnerving sense of loss. He drew water and returned to his place at the woodpile, but the effects of the young woman's mystical appearance still overwhelmed him. The others noticed his vacant stare.

"Seen a Reb, Jonah?" Shoemaker asked, recognizing his absent gape as a thing needing attention.

"No, no," he murmured, ticking his fingers against his tin cup, "but the sooner the better."

Then, as if he had willed her presence, the girl appeared in the barn's front doorway, motionless in the dancing sunlight, gazing at him. Without taking his eyes from her, he rested his empty cup on his haversack and locked his fingers under his chin, then eased his elbows to his knees. She quietly looked at him while he scrutinized her, and the others, surrendering their bread-wiped plates to Mrs. Reed, began to discuss Colonel John Hunt Morgan and his Rebel raiders, guessing the horse thief's next moves. Quiet Elias Cole said he hoped to get the bastard in his gun sight soon.

"What's the matter Jonah, ya sick?" Shoemaker pushed. "Give me yer plate, I'll take it in."

Shoemaker's nettle broke Jonah's trance. His weathered cheeks flushed imperceptibly in a rush of embarrassment. He swung around. "Thank ya John," he muttered, handing him his plate. He glanced back just in time to glimpse the young woman slip into the barn, once again swallowed by its murky shadows.

"No, no, not sick. Maybe we better be goin'," he mumbled.

The men, although brothers in their common struggle, understood the value of decisive leadership, and Jonah was a corporal now. His quiet comment had the effect of a command. The four had, without words, established a demarcation line in their relationship, the boundary where casual fellowship stops and military obligation begins. And with these men, Jonah did not need to give orders, but simply make suggestions.

"Duty calls," Fry grunted, his mustache expanding into what could be a smile, or grimace. Cole nodded as he crutched himself up with his musket.

The men thanked the Reeds for their generosity and then walked a mile to their regimental encampment in time for morning colors. Jonah never mentioned the girl to anyone.

. . . . .

Brief, testy Rebel strikes provoked spastic Federal reactions during the next four weeks, but no major offensive developed on either side. The lack of a coordinated Union response, though, provoked more than a spastic reaction in Jonah' case. His latent frustration returned to nearly conquer him. The Generals' half-hearted knee jerks were, to him, unconscionable bumbles that could win neither a battle nor the war. The minor enemy contact invariably served as a prelude to a few routine days in camp, giving everyone a chance to speculate when and where the Rebel's might jab next.

On August 17, exactly one month after Jonah's hypnotic encounter at the Reed farm, Hascall's Brigade, which included the 26th Ohio, was ordered to double back and form a defensive line west of Manchester, Tennessee. They camped only fifteen miles from the Reed farm near Shelbyville, Jonah quickly realized.

In the early evening before supper, companies C and H of the 26th were given orders to deploy at picket stations along nearby Hickory Creek. Two reliable scout reports had indicated that a Rebel battalion had deserted the area the day before, retreating north; consequently, the pickets were spaced thinly along the defensive line. The men were not allowed fires on picket duty that night, even though it was fairly certain that no enemy were present. Their haversacks bulged with a three-day load of jerky, hardtack and dried fruit. The warm August days and mild evenings made the cold rations almost enjoyable.

Facing the creek, Jonah rested his rifle against a half-rotted box elder log, spread his rubber blanket and lay down on his side. He began slicing beef jerky, watching the others settle into their positions. He could see Hickory Creek from his slightly elevated position, and although the water was seasonally low, the diminished flow still created inviting pools here and there along the cobblestone creek bed. As he chewed he studied the brook, snaking its way around gravel shoals and mud spits. The trees and bushes lining the edge of the embankment obstructed his view left and right somewhat, but he could see Sam Fry's buttocks twenty feet to his left, and to the right he found the toes of Elias Cole's boots sticking up from behind a fallen tree trunk.

He felt safe, nearly hidden in the fading light filtering through the trees and thickets, the luminescence casting shadows that served to blend his dark clothing into the shrubbery's natural contours.

From Fry's direction he heard Shoemaker's distinctive murmur; now and then Fry's grunt punctured Shoemaker's mumble, but the words were indistinguishable. He trusted his neighbors and he would sleep well in his turn. Although memories of the family farm and Sundays at church usually relaxed him for sleep, tonight his last conscious thought was of the girl he had seen at the Reed place.

Weak morning light, first light, had just begun to chase the darkness when Jonah woke with a start and stared into the gloom hanging breathless-quiet in the creekside timber. Glancing left and right he saw nothing, but sensed that the amorphous foliage still held his comrades in its murky grip. Dew damp and cool, the forest seemed paused on the final edge of tranquility, for some reason reluctant to accept the new day's life-giving light.

Listening to the sound of purling water whispering up from the creek, Jonah tried to remember what had awakened him. He looked down at the stream, and in the dull light saw the Reed girl.

Ankle-deep in a glistening pool of water, she stood facing the steep bank below him, motionless. He watched her knot her white skirts around her waist and slip to her knees, reach behind her head and begin freeing her bundled, black hair. Then, resting her hands on her thighs, she slowly bent forward, letting her hair cascade into the shimmering water. Slowly drawn under by the gently moving stream, her hair seemed to pull her forward until her forehead rippled the pool's silvery sheen.

The girl's natural symmetry and the spontaneous harmony of her movements overwhelmed Jonah. He watched her dip her pale face into the water, an instinctive baptismal cleansing, and her captured grace flowed into him as if from God, sweeping away war's unending stress and tortuous mental confusion; a distillation of absolute truth coursed through him as he watched. He felt her innocence strike to the core of his consciousness, smiting him deaf and dumb with a soundless blow, and his sense of time vanished, and he could not tell how long he lay there.

Still bent forward, the girl suddenly rose, her dripping hair glistening in the gathering light. Jonah's breath came in shallow strokes as he watched her fumble a wedge of soap from her dress' folds, ease to her knees again and began nursing the bar through her moist hair. White foam bloomed under her fingers, swelling to a rich lather that began sliding over her hands and down her black strands, finally spreading itself across the surface of the opaque pool.

Jonah lunged down the bank, splashing into the water, and the girl, unsurprised, rose when she saw him and freed her bound skirts, smoothing their wrinkles against her thighs. The two paused at arms length, looking into each other's eyes.

"Molly. Molly Reed," she whispered, turning slightly, tilting her head to one side then combing out the last droplets with her fingers.

"Jonah Hommen," he breathed, a soft gasp. She brought her head around and he stared at her pale face. He stepped forward, reaching for her shoulder, but she closed her eyes and turned away. His arm fell back to his side.

The sun's first rays suddenly broke through a gap in the thicket above them, striking their damp clothing, and her white skirts came alive. They rose to their feet. Without a word she turned to him and reached for him, and he tried to move to her but could not. In the heavy silence he again heard the brook's soft ripple.

Jonah watched the young woman wade upstream following the wooded creek bed, rippling the limpid water, her sun-struck hair glistening, her raised dress brushing her bare calves. Although the timber swallowed her too soon, the young woman's image had been etched in his mind. As she disappeared, he heard the gurgling water once more.

Jonah climbed the tangled embankment to his picket station and stood staring down at the crystal-clear pool where he had seen Molly Reed, its surface now freckled by spikes of sunlight filtering through the trees. The water spoke to him and he listened, reliving his chance encounter, a mercurial memory now dissolved in the creek's watery bosom somewhere downstream. Standing there, Jonah knew that he had captured the supreme purity of another human for the first time, a stranger, and for an instant he felt nature's vital, life-giving force seize him.

· · · · ·

Hascall's Brigade, a major element of General Buell's Army of the Ohio, slugged northwest, funneling through Purdy's Gap to an established encampment at Murfreesboro, then on to Nashville. Scouts reported that Rebel forces were massing at Gallatin, so the army then moved northeast, hounds on the scent. Although the Yankees maneuvered to confront the enemy, which matched them in number according to dependable estimates, the Rebel's customary touch-and-go tactics produced only minor contact. Chasing the Dixie ghosts, the 26th passed through Gallatin at 8 a.m. on Tuesday, September 9, 1862, without yet firing a shot, crossing into Kentucky at 10:30 a.m. the next day.

General Buell pushed his army hard, demanding his soldiers cover more ground each day in his frenzied pursuit. As the brigade pressed toward Mumfordsville, Jonah finally heard the sound of battle. Three days earlier, Union Colonel John T. Wilder had surrendered his small garrison at Mumfordsville to an overwhelming Rebel force led by General Braxton Bragg himself, and the enemy still occupied the fortified garrison. But the 26th and other regiments were not called forward to attack because it was discovered that the Confederates were withdrawing, simply fighting a delaying action at Mumfordsville. Rank and file strategists believed that the Rebels were heading north to make a major stand at Louisville, but in reality no one could know which of the Secesh slashes might be designed to cleave major Union muscle, thereby rendering the decisive bloodletting that everyone knew was sure to come.

In the early evening of Saturday, September 20,

Company C drew two days' rations instead of the usual one day draw. The double allotment told them that something more demanding than a day's march might lie ahead. "Be ready ta make the victuals last five days, boys...we'll be movin' fast an' light," Vieland warned. "Reveille at three tamarrow, maybe earlier."

The men began preparations that evening for what they expected would be, at last, a sustained Rebel encounter. The veterans quietly focused on their equipment, in reality a preoccupation serving to distract them from the looming unknown. They would turn in early tonight, knowing that insufficient rest could prove fatal. A pregnant hush fell over the camp as the experienced men went about their work, their silence serving to hone the apprehension of the newcomers.

At sundown, Jonah and Elias Cole built a frugal fire, found a scrap of wagon flooring and heaped their flour rations onto the fractured board. Cole mixed water with the white powder, palming the dough into four, foot-long snakes. The two men then wound the molded dough around green sticks and laid their caducei in the fire's hot ashes until it stiffened, then held the staves above the flame until the dough browned. They divided the bread equally.

While turning his staves over the fire, Jonah remembered the trepidation he had felt seven months earlier when he first mustered with the 26th Ohio, only a few miles from their current campsite. Since that time he had learned the ways of the army, become an effective soldier and had boldly faced the enemy. Excluding the trek through Alabama, army strategy could be seen as rational, if one allowed for the Rebels' spineless sidestepping, he conceded. He recalled his early fears at Shiloh, suddenly realizing that, after the skirmish at Corinth and his encounter with Molly Reed at Hickory Creek, he had begun to look forward to the challenge of combat.

After a supper of cooked cabbage and smoked ham, the men continued to clean their muskets and put their personal equipment in order. Quietly monitoring his soldiers, Sergeant Vieland crouched a few feet from the flickering campfire, sewing a torn canvas pouch. In a rough circle, the men of C Company passed a honing stone and a tin of gun oil among themselves; some listened to Private Shoemaker dramatize a rape case his father had defended back in Columbus. Old white male, young mulatto female. But Luke Vieland's legendary silence began to paralyze Shoemaker's glibness. Knowing that the sergeant's preoccupation cloaked an acute awareness, Shoemaker's voice rang hollow as he attempted to ease the evening's tension.

The twilight air did not cool as expected, and after Shoemaker's father established the alleged defiler's innocence, the men moved back from their cookfire, but stayed close enough to catch the dancing light. Sam Fry added unseasoned wood to the fire which oozed sap as it warmed, and then the sap ignited causing random flares, distorting and animating the gathering until it became a collection of dancing apparitions. The fire's fitful snaps and the constant click of ramrods were now the only sounds, the uncanny silence giving tomorrow's certain uncertainty a life of its own.

"Bugs're out in force tanight," Cole finally mumbled, "...maybe the stinkin' Secesh're close 'nough to be attractin' them with their smell." The rare comment swiveled a half-dozen heads, bringing a thin trail of sniggers.

Recognizing the value of humor, Shoemaker tried to enlarge the hole that Cole had punched in the blanket of tension. "Skewered three of them shiny ones on my bayonet," he announced. "Sweet an' crunchy, slow-cooked." Inspired, others stepped into the rift.

"Saw one, looked like a katydid, but bigger, carrin' off

a musket ball...musta mistook it for Yankee hardtack," someone muttered. Then from the shadows: "Don't see any vermin attackin' the officer tents over thar. Blueblood meat ain't sweet enough for 'em, I'd guess." A dozen took turns trying to top the rest, striving to flush away the combat anxiety in a whorl of humor.

Everyone knew that beneath their banter lay the bond of camaraderie, and it was time to confirm their loyalty to each other, like a last minute nod before plunging into the unknown, each man's life held in the grip of his fellow soldiers.

"I need you men to remember somethin' important."

Although Sergeant Luke Vieland's chiseled words brought instant quiet, his laconic clack turned no heads. The stillness, a profound, underwater swimmer's silence, grew heavy, broken only by the click of ramrods and the fire's pop and sizzle.

"There's not a man here I don't trust," he finally said. "Ya'll know yer business, learnt it under enemy fire. Maybe I don't recognize what's in yer head time ta time, but whatever's thar, it's sufficient fer the fight. From now on, if ya need ta make a decision in battle, stand by it. Don't wait fer me no more. Trust yerself."

Sergeant Vieland gathered his trappings, rose to his feet, shouldered his bedroll and strode into the darkness without looking back. The deadly quiet lingered. Shoemaker swung his musket to his lap, glancing around at his comrades.

"Damn. What the hell was that all about?" he asked, locking onto Sam Fry. "The sergeant leavin' us, or what?"

"Don't think so, John," Fry answered. "I think he jest wants to give us a compliment and don't know how. What you think, Elias?"

"What religion is he?" Cole asked, ignoring Fry's drift.

"He said he don't have none, once," Shoemaker blurted.

Jonah stood and turned to Cole.

"He don't need one, but I think the rest of us better pray real good in church come Sunday!" Jonah boomed, his voice resonating in the stillness like a prophetic warning, his grave tone surprising even himself.

Jonah lay awake that night pondering Vieland's words, wondering what decisions a soldier like himself could possibly make on the battlefield. He remembered their last scrap with Forrest's cavalry at McMinnville, how easily the enemy had escaped, as if by plan. He remembered Sergeant Vieland ordering them to hit the mud and shoot. Recounting the incident produced a sudden malaise. Sergeant Vieland had always seen that they took the right positions, did the right thing, and that was as it should be, and nothing should change it.

Jonah realized that throughout his life he had relied on the example of his father and community leaders, and in the army he had found a comfortable niche under Sergeant Vieland's wing. But now he recognized in Vieland's words a mandate for independence, and it frightened him. He lay quietly trying to focus the lens of introspection, examine the cause of his sudden dread. A dark, blurry image of total autonomy blinked his eyes.

· · · · ·

Relevant Diary Entries

Thurs July 17th 1862
Reveille at 3 A.M., and started on the march at 7, without any breakfast we marched two miles above Shelbyville and encamped at 1 ½ P.M. We took breakfast at 3 P.M. Our Co went on picket

Friday July 18th
I and J Shoemaker and W. S. Grubaugh got our breakfast at Mr Reeds We were relieved by Co A at 8 oclock and came into camp I washed in the afternoon. We had nothing to eat.

Sun Aug 17th
Reveille at 3 A.M. and marched at daylight. We encamped at hickory creek. Co C went on picket.

Sat Sept 6th
We marched at 4 A.M, and marched 22 miles and encamped at noon 2 miles from Nashville. The road is crowded with troops all the p.m. We passed through a town by the name of Lavarn 15 miles from Nashville at 8 A.M.

Mond Sept 8th
We started on the march again at sunrise and marched within 3 miles of Galatin and encamped, there is a rebel force reported at G.

Tues Sept 9th
We marched at 6 A.M. We passed through Galatin at 8. and encamped after dark

Wed Sept 10th **1862**
We marched at daylight We passed through Michelville at 10 A.M. We crossed the Ten and Ky line at 10 ½. We passed through Franklin at noon We encamped at 4 P.M. and took supper and marched again at 9 P.M. We passed through Woodville at 10 P.M. We went within three miles of Bowling Green and encamped

Tues Sept 16th
We received marching orders at noon and started at 3 P.M.

We went above town and forded barren river We encamped at Camp Robinson at 9 P.M. Capt Ross took Command of Co C this P.M.

Wed Sept 17th

We marched at 7 A.M. and encamped 5 miles from Bells tavern. There was skirmishing in front all day. It rained all the evening

Thurs Sept 18th

We marched at daylight There was skirmishing again in front We marched 10 miles and encamped at 10 A.M. We heard of Co Wylders surrender at Mumfordsville. We marched again at 3 P.M. and encamped at Cave City The 1st Ky Cavalry had a skirmish here this P.M. and captured 70 prisoners. Co C went on picket.

Sat Sept 20th

We had battalion drill in the A.M. Elias Cole and I went out in the country We received two days rations to last us five, and had orders to march at 3 A.M. We mixed up our flour with water and baked it in the ashes and on boards, and wound it around staves and held it before the fire

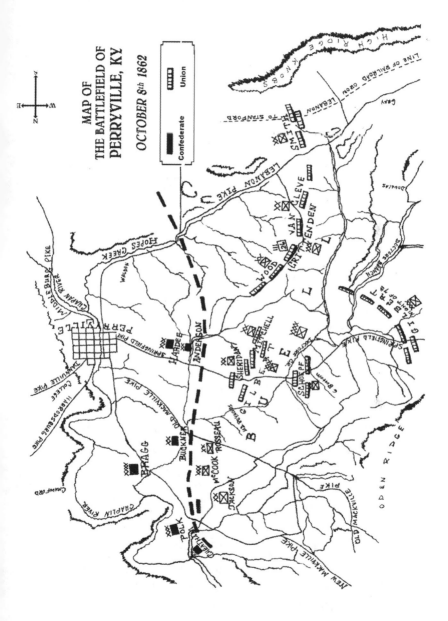

MAP OF
THE BATTLEFIELD OF
PERRYVILLE, KY
OCTOBER 8th 1862

Confederate

Union

6.

*"But as they sailed...there came down a storm of wind...
and...they were...in jeopardy." Luke 8:23*

The bugler at regimental headquarters barked an emphatic
reveille at 3:15 a.m., but Jonah did not stir. Even when Sam
Fry, his tent mate, tugged on his boots, crawled over him and
stomped out toward the latrine, the commotion had no effect
on Jonah's slumber. His eyes finally popped open on the last
note of breakfast call but he lay still, staring into the darkness.
The rattle of mess gear told him he might be in trouble.

He snatched his metal plate and spoon from his
haversack and leapt from the dog tent, knocking away
Fry's musket, which had been stuck in the ground by its
bayonet to support one end of the shelter. He sat on the
collapsed canvas, jerked on his boots then stumbled toward
the cookfire winking at him through the trees.

After hardtack, bacon and grits, Company C broke camp
and joined the regiment alongside the road, but no orders
came. The men milled around for half an hour, finally shed
their gear and sat on it while watching a cluster of officers

talk quietly, occasionally retrieving papers and maps from their saddled horses.

Finally, amid a flurry of urgent commands, Hascall's Brigade moved out at six a.m., first light, at the doublequick. After 30 minutes of hard running, the 26th left the pike without breaking stride, rolling into a line of battle on the right of the brigade. Colonel Fyffe galloped ahead, suddenly raised his right arm and slid his mount to a stop on the wet turf. The line of men heaved and halted just in time to hear three batteries of Union artillery cut loose behind them. After two barrages, the brigade struck out again, this time at the rout step, and now Mumfordsville lay only a mile in front, but they heard no enemy fire.

Just as Company C crested a hill above Green River, a squad of Rebel cavalry, which apparently had been guarding the railroad bridge spanning the river in front of the town, opened fire with small arms, and then spun around to gallop off under a hail of Yankee lead.

"*They spit thar whole quid!*" Shoemaker shouted, reloading. "Hefty spew, but they didn't hit a damn thing!" he added, narrating the event for those who might not be paying attention.

"Neither did we," Fry grumbled.

Suddenly a Secesh battery, hidden in a timbered swale across the river, opened up, their shells bursting in front and behind the company. The men dove for cover just in time to watch the Rebel's wheel their guns around and scramble away like frightened deer, melting into the woods.

Hot on the heels of the retreating Southerners, the men swept forward on Sergeant Vieland's order, fording the stream under the railroad bridge in order to have cover from counter-attack while they waded the waist-deep water. Once on the opposite side, they reformed and marched at the quicktime straight toward town, catching up with the retreating 3rd Ohio Cavalry which was engaged with a swarm of Southern horsemen twice its number. The Rebel cavalry saw the Federal infantry coming, reeled, spun around and galloped hell-bent-for-leather down the Louisville Pike, twisting in their saddles now and then to fire side arms at the charging Yankees. "Recall" sounded, then "assembly", and the men formed ranks just north of town.

The 26th dug itself into perimeter defensive positions north of Mumfordsville all afternoon, but marched back into town to camp at the railway depot just before dark. The previous February, Jonah had been in the railroad station building on his way to the regiment; now its windows had been shot out and a huge hole in the roof gave the structure an all-too-airy ambiance. Many of the men fell asleep before they could eat supper, but Jonah consumed a half-ration, realizing that he had better stoke the coals while he had a chance. He ate with his back against a brick wall then slid down along the wall, tucked his haversack under his head and fell instantly asleep.

The next morning, the regiment moved out smartly at first light and marched into Elizabethtown at sundown, covering half the distance, thirty miles, at the quicktime. Having left the wagons carrying their tents and baggage far behind, they slept in the open. Every last soldier knew his mission—get to Louisville, drive the Rebels out of the city.

The leading elements of General Buell's army reached West Point on the Ohio River the next day, a twenty-four mile trek without food for Company C. The advance units, which included Hascall's Brigade, were ordered to keep going, even though the sun had set. A twenty-mile night march got them to the outskirts of Louisville at 3 a.m. on the following day, September 25, a Thursday Jonah would remember as the day he was delivered to the halls of heaven, albeit a short stay. The brigade rested until seven a.m., ate a cold breakfast and then formed by regiment to start their parade into town.

Lining the streets six deep, exuberant citizens began cheering and waving as soon as the soldiers came into view; some threw bright ribbons and flowers at them as they passed. The Rebels had nearly sacked their city, and the Federal army's timely arrival had saved them from complete ruin. The men marched down the street like "swaggering Zouave," according to John Shoemaker, whose head snapped around every time he heard a woman's cheering voice. "Two days ago ya was too tired ta chase flies off yer food, John," Fry mumbled, "but look at ya now...wild dog hungry an' moonshine wild."

"You boys danced the bastards home!" an old man yelled from the crowd, but his enthusiastic praise was not entirely accurate. Rumors of Rebel activity had circulated in camp that morning, accounts of how the Secesh had not retreated but were regrouping at Bardstown, only 50 miles southeast. The people lining the streets, though, celebrated as if the war had ended when the Rebels deserted Louisville.

The town's ladies, dressed in their finest raiment for the victory parade–colorful hats and hoop skirts trimmed with lacy scallops–did an excellent job keeping their heroes' eyes spinning in their sockets. Jonah glanced at Fry, alongside. "Quit gawkin' Sam, yer brains might fall out yer mouth," he grunted. Sam Fry had riveted on an endangered display of cleavage boldly leaning from a second story window. "I think they did already," he gasped.

Cole could not resist. "Sure they did, Sam, and I stepped on 'em, but it weren't more 'n steppin' on a dried walnut."

"I wonder if all them ladies're taken?" Shoemaker wheezed, seeming to briefly recover from a sustained trance.

"*Eyes front thar!*" a voice of unknown origin commanded from behind, and the men snapped into alignment. But the dressed ranks and files did not last long. As the parade passed the courthouse, people deep in the crowd pushed forward, throwing those in front into the soldiers, creating rifts in their ranks. The men recovered and forged ahead, their moist eyeballs whirling and ricocheting like bees in a glass jar.

The 26th bivouacked outside the city at the end of Third Street; their equipment and supply wagons caught up with them just before sundown.

On Friday morning, the four musketeers, Jonah, Fry, Cole, and Shoemaker, went together to sign the payrolls at headquarters. Although it was raining a soft drizzle, after lunch the four walked a mile to the 121st and found Fry's cousins from Marion County, Jarvis Aldrich and Charles Holt. That evening, the six went into town and ate an oyster supper, a thing unimagined on their race to save Louisville.

After supper, Jonah and Sam Fry went to the theater to see *The Marble Heart*, a popular play well advertised by posters and handbills. There, Jonah found himself in another world. Before him the story unfolded, a tale conceived in the mind of a playwright, a threatless fantasy that Jonah could watch without involvement; yet, it became a part of his world while he sat safely in his seat, simply watching. The gaslights flared and the performance ended too soon.

The men drew their pay the next day, twelve dollars for Shoemaker, Cole and Fry, and thirteen for Jonah. Nume Barber, Elias Cole's half-brother from Company B, joined them, and the five moneyed soldiers "skedaddled" to the market to buy fresh produce. The permanent market stalls had sold out, but produce-laden farm wagons were arriving steadily. As soon as the wagon's tailgates dropped, a swarm of soldiers descended on them. The men found ripe tomatoes, carrots, snapping beans, celery and onions, but had to be quick to claim their stake before it disappeared.

Each bought a large quantity of one item and shared with the rest. Starved for fresh produce, the men had not been able to forage for greens in the field because of the fast pace. And lately the farmers had begun to plant their vegetable gardens close to their houses in order to see which army was confiscating their crops. Further, the rascal farmers sometimes guarded their treasure with loaded shotguns.

The soldiers walked to the railroad station's loading dock and sat on a cargo dolly before beginning the feast, which ended in only twenty minutes when the food ran out. After the feeding frenzy, Jonah bought a newspaper and read it aloud while his companions drank coffee on the depot platform.

The Louisville *Courier* praised General Rosecrans' victory at Iuka, Mississippi, a battle won against a superior Rebel force led by General Sterling Price. But the editor was not laudatory in his article describing Indiana General Jeff C. Davis' murderous pistol shot that killed Union General William Nelson at the Galt House in Louisville.

"Shootin's one way to settle an argument, but it's unchristian outside a fight in the field," Jonah declared, adding, "name callin' or no name callin'." Elias Cole, at his laconic best, cut to the core of matter.

"It's a bad example fer the men, the sin of it hid under honor," he said.

Shoemaker nodded but said nothing, seeming distracted, as if he were ruminating over a strategy for General Davis' defense in court.

Jonah visualized Reverend Sable back home, eyes burning and fist thumping as he addressed the morality of wrongful revenge. He tried to imagine how the preacher would compare the generals' carnal passion with The Great Cause. Jonah concluded that the killing, a prideful murder, would no doubt go unpunished. General Davis would not stand trial if he could show that his honor had been violated, as Cole had suggested.

On Tuesday, Jonah offered to buy theater tickets for those who could not afford them. Sam Fry immediately decided to see *The Marble Heart* again. Paying their own way, Shoemaker and Cole joined their stage-addicted companions for a night of diversion, and the four arrived early to join a crowd waiting for the theater doors to open. Two civilians stood in front of them. The larger man appeared as if he had swallowed a watermelon, his vest stretching over his stomach like a sow's hide drying on a barrel. From their conversation, Jonah deduced that the big man owned a bank, and his friend, a small fellow with a chipmunk face, apparently ran the mercantile emporium over on Chestnut Street.

"The hired help saved our bacon this time," the chipmunk chirped, flashing a smile at his friend, seeming not to notice the soldiers standing behind.

"The musket bumpkins?"

"The hayseeds."

"Can't thank 'em enough," the banker barked. "I don't need any Rebel withdrawals right now. Since the scare passed, deposits have picked up real nice."

"Well, the relief helped the dry goods business too. At least the Yankees pay for what they take. But, if I'm gonna have an even chance, the boys better drive 'em south and keep 'em there."

"Even chance, ha!" the big man grumbled, "you're gettin' an even chance, all right. Everyone needs general merchandise, war or no war, but dealin' in money, like I do, is a different matter. The bigger the scare, the more the withdrawals. And the less I have to work with, the less the profit there is. Maybe the fightin'll move further south an' give me a chance to make some solid rebuildin' loans."

"Well, I hope you're right, Robert. To tell the truth,

my store's doing as well now as it ever did…steady volume even with the higher prices. The demand's got to continue, though, so I can meet the rising wholesale prices without lookin' for one of your loans."

"Actually, it'd suit me if the war lasted awhile," said the banker, "with deposits from fellas like you growin' every day. Opportunity knocks only once, they say. The war keeps business profitable, and that's good for everyone, in my view."

Shoemaker had heard enough. Never bashful, he broke in, his voice slicing through the ambient hubbub like a bugle call:

"What'd you fellers do, buy substitutes with yer war booty so's you can stay home an' rob the women folk?"

The two spun around to see John looming above them. Heated to a boil, Shoemaker knocked their stovepipes to the cobblestones with a swift sweep of his arm.

"I never smelt hog slop like yer makin'!" he rasped. "You think good men oughta get shot up so's the likes of you can get rich? What ya mean, 'we're' fighting the war? Who? Not you chiselers, that's fer damn sure!"

The two bareheaded civilians stood staring at the soldiers, their minds whirring, the tension tactile.

Suddenly the civilians picked up their hats, turned away and broke through the crowd. Cole and Shoemaker flexed open their clenched fists, and Jonah noticed that Fry's face had become a tornado again, waxed mustache twisted, dark eyes flashing.

Jonah asked himself if, had it become necessary, he would have fought with his comrades. He concluded he would have, having forgotten the morality issue he had attached to the fighting generals at the Galt House.

. . . . .

The regiment struck out southeast on the Bardstown Pike at noon on Wednesday October 1ˢᵗ, leading the way straight at the enemy. But the next day the 26ᵗʰ remained in camp to watch the infantry regiments that had been behind them march ahead. After breakfast, Captain Meredith went to regimental headquarters to confirm his orders, but did not return. A messenger said that the captain had gone home sick. His replacement, Captain William Ross, took command of Company C the same day. The regiment marched at noon.

From then on, whenever there was firing in front, Captain Ross galloped straightaway toward the noise for a look-see. When he returned he always conferred with Sergeant Vieland, apparently to confirm his conclusions, or get the sergeant's ideas about how the company might be deployed under the conditions, had the incident become a fight.

They passed through Mount Washington on Friday October 3ʳᵈ, camping that afternoon on the Salt River. Heavy cannonading to the east boomed all evening. Moving fast and light again, everyone knew things were heating up, and guessed that the pot was about to boil over. They were right. The next day it did.

Reveille sounded at 4 a.m. and they threw on their traps without eating, but did not march until 6 a.m., the 26ᵗʰ once more leading the brigade. To Jonah's surprise, the entire brigade left the main pike at ten o'clock and lay in the woods only a mile from Fairfield. While the men hid in the shade to avoid the scorching sun, Sergeant Vieland moved among them, ordering water conservation and murmuring a few words of encouragement. Then, without warning, Jonah's regiment and the 58ᵗʰ Indiana were sent forward. With no water available and little left among the troops, the men began to suffer in the terrible heat wave that had descended and steadily grown worse since Louisville. The few creeks and drainage runs they crossed as they moved through the fields lay baking in the sun, their beds powder-dry.

Suddenly the sharp rake of massed musketry swept through a stand of trees ahead, apparently from the opposite side of the woods. Captain Ross galloped forward, and the men, packed tight in line of battle, followed him, stumbling into the trees at the doublequick. They dashed to the brow of a wooded hill but saw only cleared farmland in front of them. Then, from the woods opposite the fields, Federal cavalry came back on the run, straight at them, but when the horse soldiers saw the Yankee infantry break from the trees ahead of them they rallied, forming quickly for a charge. Two batteries of Federal artillery rolled up through the woods behind the 26th, punching holes in the Union line of battle as they ran ahead, hot on the heels of the reorganized cavalry. As the 26th swept down the hill toward the cleared fields, the Rebels came out of the woods on the far side. The Federal infantry advanced steadily, kneeling to fire over their charging cavalry below them. The Rebels, stunned by the coordinated Yankee attack, turned and ran like scared deer, flying through Bardstown and down the Danville Pike.

The regiment camped in the Catholic churchyard on the outskirts of Bardstown at sundown, and, although exhausted, Jonah could not sleep. He lay awake for over an hour. In spite of their best efforts, little had been accomplished in the field that day. The old malaise began to rear its ugly head. He finally prayed, asking God to make the Rebels stop running and give up. Soon after the prayer his dark frustration began to lift and he drifted asleep.

The next morning Captain Ross invited Sergeant Vieland, Sam Fry and Jonah into town for breakfast. A wiry fellow of about twenty-five years, Ross came from Marion, Ohio, where he and his father both taught school. But the captain did not carry himself like a preoccupied scholar, rather more like a hardened Texas cowpoke well aware of his surroundings, bowed legs and all. His smaller than average stature belied his sinewy toughness. They settled around one of several tables set out on the boardwalk in front of the Bleaker Hotel.

After they ate their eggs and jellied bread, Captain Ross glanced at his watch, then the sun. "Since June," he said, "the sun's been spinning toward its winter solstice over the Tropic of Capricorn, in the Southern Hemisphere. Since then," he added, "the days have been getting shorter. When the sun gets over the equator on its way south," he told them, "it's called the autumnal equinox, and that happened last month…as it does every September." He sipped his coffee and returned Sam Fry's stare.

"Hit's highest in June then, Captain?" Fry asked.

"That's right," Ross said, flashing a smile.

"How come hit's so damn hot now, then, Captain, hotter 'an June?"

Ross smiled again. "This year God's scorching a few Rebel backsides to make 'em run faster." The men chuckled.

But Jonah had already learned of the sun's path from Reverend Sable during Bible study. Sergeant Vieland, too, seemed to understand celestial affairs, nodding as Captain Ross spoke. The fact that Sergeant Vieland seemed to know about equinoxes and solstices surprised Jonah.

"We'll get some rain soon, I think…that'll finish the heat," Vieland clipped, looking at Sam Fry and adding, "an' next month we'll all be wishin' for a little warm weather." But for Jonah, less daylight meant that the chances of confronting the enemy were getting slimmer, and the thought began to distress him. Winter days, if the war lasted that long, were too short, too short to settle anything.

The division band serenaded the troops out of

Bardstown at 11 o'clock the same morning, the cautious Yankees following in the warm wake of retreating General Bragg and his consolidated Confederate army.

The 26th camped at Beach Fork that night, then at the Springfield Fair Grounds the following evening, where they watched 1200 Federal cavalry pass by, moving ahead of them. On Tuesday, October 7th, the Yankees marched at 11 a.m. and it got hot as hell's kitchen again, and water could be found nowhere. But the Federal army pressed on, passing through Haysville at midnight, finally stopping at 3 a.m.

After two hours rest, reveille sounded at five, and while the men ate cold rations in the dark, they heard mounted officers galloping through camp. At first light they formed four abreast on the pike and immediately heard the rattle and slash of musket volleys a short distance ahead. Colonel Fyffe assembled his officers alongside the road. When Captain Ross returned to his company he told Sergeant Vieland to dismiss the men and hold them at their campsite until 11 a.m. They sat until noon listening to the tremendous roar of battle, cannon and musketry duels taking place left and right. Finally the regiment swept into a line of battle and moved forward, but had only a brief exchange of fire with retreating Rebels. Most of the army had fought blistering engagements that day, but the 26th, held in reserve, saw little action. They lay awake in a line of battle throughout the night while the rest of the army slept.

The Federal victory over the Confederates at Perryville that day would be the most decisive battle fought in Kentucky. The fight won praise from all corners of the Union, but not from Jonah Hommen.

"Why couldn't we snare the skunk at Perryville?" he asked at breakfast two days later.

"The critter stepped over the trap," Cole grumbled.

"But we shot his ass off," Shoemaker surged, "an' he'll

bleed to death 'fore Christmas."

Jonah stood guard at division headquarters the following day and learned that General Buell had mustered nearly 37,000 men for the battle, while Confederate General Bragg had deployed only 16,000. The following night Jonah lay awake in a fruitless line of battle, listening to Sam Fry snore next to him, trying to make sense of the facts he had gathered at headquarters. The Union had suffered more than forty-two hundred killed, wounded or vanished, he remembered, and the Rebels lost only thirty-three hundred. How can we call that a victory? Bragg might not be the smartest man in the world, but can Buell be any smarter, losing so many? Does whoever *says* he wins, actually win? If the dead men from both sides were right, then the Union has the honor of being the most right, since we got the most men killed, he reasoned. Anger kept him awake nearly all night.

Company C rousted itself from its line of battle at sunup and assembled on Captain Ross, but Sergeant Luke Vieland did not get up. The company commander called for the surgeon.

· · · · ·

Relevant Diary Entries

Sunday Sept 21ˢᵗ/62
Reveille at 3 A.M. and marched at 6. We went up the pike one mile and our division deployed to the right and moved up in line of battle until one P.M. when the division again came on the pike and kept on towards Mumfordsville. We came up to the fortification by the R.R. bridge, where we found a squad of rebel cavalry We soon routed them, when a sharp cannonading took place with the rebel battery on the hill across the river. There was some shells bursted in

our Co but did no harm. We then started on and forded the river by the bridge and doublequicked up to town where the 3rd O cavalry was fighting. When the rebels saw us coming over the hill they retreated on the Louisville pike we encamped out by the depot at dark

Tues 23rd 1862
We marched at 5 A.M. and rested at on P.M. 1 ½ miles from Elizabethtown We marched again at 7 P.M. and encamped at 2 A.M. We had nothing to eat.

Wed Sept 24th 1862
We marched at 5 A.M. and arrived at West Point on the Ohio river at 1 A.M. I went over on the Ind side. We marched again at 5 P.M. and went up the river three miles and encamped

Thurs Sept 25. 1862
We marched at 8 A.M. and went up the pike 8 miles and then turned off the road and went down to the river and encamped and took supper. We marched again at 8 P.M. and arrived at Louisville at 3 A.M.

Fri Sept 26th
Jim Rugh and I went up in town in the A.M. We signed the pay rolls in the P.M. and James Goodman and I went up to the 121st

Sat Sept 27th
Sam Fry and I went to market in the morning. We moved our camp at 10 A.M. just outside the city on third street. It was rainy the most of the afternoon. I went up to the 121st and Jarvis Aldrich, Charles Holt and I went down in town and got an Oyster supper. Sam Fry and I went to the theater this evening

Mond Sept 29
There is nothing going on in camp. Gen Nelson was shot this morning by Gen Jeff C. Davis of Ind J.L. Hall and I was up to market this morning

Tues Sept 30ᵗʰ 1862
John Shoemaker, Nume Barber and I went up in town this A.M. We received marching orders with orders to have 3 days rations in our haversacks. John Hall and I went to the theater this evening

Wednesday Oct 1ˢᵗ 1862
We marched at 9 A.M. and left the city at noon on the Bardstown pike. We marched 11 miles and encamped at Paupan hill

Frid Oct 3ʳᵈ 1862
We were called up at 3 A.M. and put on our traps, and remained until daylight. We marched at 8 A.M. We passed through Mt Washington at noon We encamped on salt river There was cannonading to our right this P.M.

Saturday Oct 4ᵗʰ
Reveille at 4 A.M. and marched at 6 Our Regt was in the advance. We left the main pike and went by the way of Fairfield when we got within 1 ½ miles of the fair ground we encamped, but our Regt and the 58ᵗʰ Ind was sent on ahead. We soon heard heavy musketry in front we started on in double quick and as we came up to the brow of the hill, our cavalry came back on the run, but when they seen us coming up they ralyed again The artillery ran ahead and Our Regt formed line on the right, and sent out skirmishers. And after a short cannonading we moved forward, and the rebels retreated through Bardstown and left on the Danville

pike. We got into town at sundown and encamped in the Catholic church yard. There was geat enthusiasm among the Citizens where we came in.

Sunday Oct 5th
Capt Ross, Sam Fry and I went and got our breakfast. We marched at 11 A.M. and encamped on beach fork at 10 P.M.

Mond Oct 6th
We marched at Sunrise We halted at 10 A.M. to let 1200 cavalry pass. We encamped at Springfield at 4 P.M. We camped in the fair ground

Tues Oct 7th 1862
We marched at 11 A.M. the day was very hot and water scarce We passed through Haysville at midnight and encamped at 3 A.M.

Wed Oct 8th 1862
We laid in camp until 11 A.M. and then marched up in front of Parysville. A part of our division was in the fight but Our Regt was held as reserve. We laid in line of battle through the night.

Thurs Oct 9th 1862
We marched into the pike at 2 P.M. and went through Parysville and encamped on the battle field one mile from town.

7.

"And he led them out as far as to Bethany, and he lifted up his hands, and blessed them. And it came to pass, while he blessed them, he was parted from them, and carried up into heaven." Luke 24:50,51

Inexplicably, the Union juggernaut paused at Perryville, giving the Confederates an opportunity to recoil southeast and time to regroup. The hiatus also allowed the Federals' support wagons to catch up with the main body; the teamsters stopped a half-mile behind the infantry's hastily dug entrenchments. The surgeon's ambulance, a two-wheeled, mule-drawn shay, arrived at C Company only fifteen minutes after it was summoned.

The corpulent doctor's spectacles glinted in the emerging sunlight as he laboriously climbed down then waddled toward the men gathered around their sergeant. The soldiers jostled a pathway for him; he quickly brushed through them and knelt alongside Luke Vieland, who lay on his stomach. The surgeon began examining the sergeant's head and neck, sending off a series of wheezes as he explored. He then paused, brushed his hand over his close-cropped beard. With some effort he rose to his feet and reached for a black satchel that the ambulance driver, a mere boy, had carried from the wagon.

"Would you please remove the clothing?" the doctor asked, addressing no one in particular.

Privates Shotwell and Bradfield rolled Luke Vieland to his back and began to unbuckle and unbutton, a hesitant, labored undertaking, finally pulling free his uniform and boots. The surgeon drew a circle in the air with his forefinger, and the two men gently returned Vieland to his stomach.

Startled by the milky whiteness of the sergeant's well-muscled body, Jonah thought for an instant that there had been a mistake in identity. The innocent-looking flesh seemed to belong to another species, a creature apart from the temporal world and God's restorative sunlight. But the sergeant's swarthy hands and face were unmistakable. The doctor examined Vieland's backside, parted his buttocks, glimpsed, cautiously turned him over, spread his legs and extended his subject's arms straight out at shoulder level, all the while inspecting him carefully.

The moment that the surgeon had begun to turn the body, Jonah heard Vieland's piercing command, "*Roll!*" explode in his head, and he felt the crush of instant anger. *The sergeant knows when ta move, how ta move, and don't want ta move now! Leave him be!*

The medic fished a silver spoon from his satchel, kneeled and teased it down the cadaver's throat. He peered inside. *Shame upon you! Maulin' a helpless man! Stop. Dammit stop! Maybe I'll...maybe I'll....*

The soldiers watched the doctor bring Vieland's legs together, so that the body formed a cross, instantly reminding Jonah of an eagle poised on the edge of flight, its ebony plumage defined by a border of white feathers along its wings. Then Jonah remembered the cadavers at Shiloh, their parting ghosts, white vapor balls that had proved death, making it certain, but no apparition swirled above Vieland's body. *Maybe he isn't....* Desperation suddenly swept through Jonah. *Stop, dammit, stop! Keep away!* Jonah's muscles tingled as he crouched in front of Vieland, gripping his musket barrel. He could not move.

The absence of an external wound seemed to perplex the doctor, a scientist by nature. He finally hefted himself to his feet and hovered above the body, scanning it again, and then Captain Ross asked him if the sergeant was officially dead. The men fixed on the doctor. "Yes, yes," he grumbled, glancing at Ross, "dead as a man gets."

Would the surgeon examine beneath the skin? Jonah asked himself. Perform an autopsy? No, not here. On the battlefield, Jonah realized, only enemy shot make incisions.

As the surgeon turned to leave, the men pressed forward, jostling him without apology, nearly blocking his escape. Their grievous faces demanded something, an answer that might allay their rising trepidation. Kneeling motionless at the corpse's feet, Jonah heard Vieland's words at the Mumfordsville camp, only eighteen days earlier:

"Don't wait fer me no more. Trust yerself."

A mercurial fear fluttered through Jonah, and for an instant the breath of panic touched his stomach. The surgeon looked at Captain Ross.

"May I ask you to have your men assist my driver in wrapping the sergeant's body in a blanket and carrying it to the shay, Captain?"

"Yes sir, you may."

No one moved.

"Well, then?"

Ross tossed his head, a signal to do as the doctor asked, and backed away.

Fry tucked his ground cloth around Vieland, and then

he, Shotwell and Cole shouldered the shrouded corpse and lurched toward the ambulance. The rest trailed in their wake, a somber, hushed cortege, its shuffling boots raising dust motes to sparkle in the brilliant morning light.

The soldiers watched as the shay, Vieland's body strapped to the luggage rack in back, crawled toward the road, and then C Company fell into ranks on Captain Ross' command. At quicktime, they caught up with the regiment, marched back through Perryville, circled and finally camped in mid-afternoon on the torn battleground, one mile west of town.

No one spoke of Vieland's death that afternoon, it simply hung over them like the blade of a guillotine waiting for a wrong word to trigger its fall. They did not know how or why Vieland had died, or where his body might be buried, but they somehow accepted the frustration of having to defer their pointless, but critical, questions. That evening as they sat around their fires, the fact that their mentor was lost forever tore into them like a firing squad's volley. A pall settled over their sepulcheral supper like a black hood slipping over the head of the condemned. A suffocating silence ebbed and flowed in rhythm with the tide of darkness as it crept, all too soon, into their camp.

The evening's pleasant coolness nuzzled Jonah as he fluffed out his bedroll and collapsed on his coarse wool blanket, but he ignored what solace nature might offer. The men's incessant coughing, hacking, and murmuring unnerved him. He felt closed in and watched, as if someone were lurking behind a nearby tree, judging, criticizing, about to demand something of him, and he did not know who might be doing this or what they could want, or why he felt the way he did. He longed to be alone, slumbering in an uncomplicated, predictable wilderness. He cursed his promotion to corporal.

Jonah's own words, spoken just before his first skirmish

at Corinth, coursed through him as he lay quietly: *Ya could be angry. I think anger takes over scared.* He fought to recapture his conviction. *Scared? Who's scared?* he asked himself. But the haunting malaise, the fear of fear, would not leave. The need to be alone, find the root of his desertion fear, dispel his sense of impending doom, gnawed in his shrinking stomach. He blinked into the gathering darkness, remembering when he was a ten year-old boy coming home to find the house empty. The sting of desertion began to crystallize in his stomach. Emotional pain dried his mouth. He reached for his canteen.

Night finally fell, snuffing autumn's feckless twilight with a wink. In the somber starlight Jonah watched a shaft of gray campfire smoke rise to form a dark canopy under the trees then slowly filter skyward to challenge the windless heavens. Through a gap in the branches he saw the silver moon prick a neat hole in the black sky and searched the branches for twinkling stars, all the while listening to soft snores compete with the random murmurs of men still awake. A soft breeze began to nudge the smoke layered under the trees, coaxing it up into the white moonlight, and he finally slept.

. . . . .

First light on October 10, a rainy Friday, brought the muffled thumps of distant artillery duels thudding through the heavy air. The Ohio soldiers mustered on the muddy Danville road without breakfast. But as the regiment marched out, the ominous rumble suddenly fell silent. The troops left the road to camp in a walnut grove only a mile and a half downroad from their earlier bivouac, leaving the men of Company C with yet another day for rumination.

In the middle of breakfast the next morning, a Confederate scouting party, which had apparently become suicidal, attacked a thin line of poorly spaced Union pickets, collapsing them to within sight of the regiment's camp. The startled Yankee infantry raked two hasty volleys across the advancing Rebels, four of the Federal artillery shells bursting dead center among the band of yelping Southerners. Six Secesh, three dead and three seriously wounded, were unable to turn and run with the rest. The 26th finished their meal and routinely deployed to a defensive line, lying in their positions throughout the day.

Settling behind a hollow log, Jonah suddenly realized that his anxiety had disappeared during the early morning brush with the enemy. The unforeseen clash had cleared his head, focused him. The broken breakfast, he reasoned, had made it possible to compare himself with himself, before and after the skirmish. He had crawled out that morning confused and unsure, but when the Rebels struck he knew what was expected of him and did precisely that, and his concentration on the fight had cleansed his mind. But as he lay thinking, the fragile respite, the mental peace the skirmish had delivered, slowly evaporated. He languished in line of battle that day, anxiety once again crawling over him like a chilling fog.

On Monday, two miles south of Danville, Jonah took his turn on guard duty at division headquarters, a welcomed relief from the hot, demanding chase. Pacing back and forth in front of a stockaded Sibley, he could hear staff officers just inside the tent criticizing General Buell's strategy, especially the general's inclination to simply nip the heels of Bragg's retreating Rebels. Buell's subordinate commanders complained of bursts of doublequick marches in order to gain questionable position, and all-too-frequent countermarches. Their lack of confidence angered Jonah at first, but at supper he remembered that he, too, longed to end the chase and confront the enemy. The thought that his yearning was shared by divisional officers brought momentary comfort.

At 1 a.m. the next morning, the 26th moved out toward Stanford, Kentucky, without Jonah, who was asleep in the guards' A tent at division headquarters. Fighting for oxygen in the fumed tent, which had become rank with the trapped breath of five men spooned together, Jonah woke at 5 a.m. to hear the rattle of the division commander's equipment and furniture being loaded into wagons.

At sunrise, after the guards finished a breakfast of cold ham mixed with rice, the sergeant major dismissed them, giving Jonah directions to his unit. He struck out on the Stanford road, reaching the town at noon.

"Have ya seen the Twenty-sixth Infantry?" he asked a middle-aged dandy dressed like a riverboat gambler, who was busy watering three saddled horses in front of the saloon. The fellow wore a constable's badge pinned to his vest. It flashed in the sunlight as he spoke.

"Yep. They ran through town two hours ago, soldier, 'long with the Fifty-eighth. Headed southeast. You'll never catch 'em."

Oddly, the peace officer's measured certainty resurrected Jonah's fear of desertion. He turned and jogged down the road with his musket at port arms, scrambling to escape his feelings as much as to catch up. Two hours later he found his friends laying in line of battle, having just concluded a brief, yet intense skirmish.

Jonah threw himself into position behind a felled tree with Elias Cole on the left and John Ashburn, now the company clerk, and John Shoemaker on his right. They watched him tamp his musket and settle in, saying nothing.

"Sorry I missed it," he grunted, rolling to his stomach, still sucking breath from the run.

"You sure?" Shoemaker grumbled.

"I need the relief…a good fracas now an' again, I

mean."

"I don't," Cole clipped, his eyes searching the thick underbrush forming a screen only twenty yards straight ahead.

The next day, after a bloody, ten-minute clash at Crab Orchard in which three men of the 58th Indiana were killed and a half-dozen of the 26th were wounded, Jonah once again tried to make sense of his compulsion to seek mental peace in the fight. It was an illogical thing, but he could not deny his desperate need to risk his life in order to relax his snarled intestines. Mulling over the dilemma, he realized that the introspective process itself might be missing something crucial, maybe a fundamental truth that the others had discovered and digested, but kept to themselves. How *did* the others find acceptance of Vieland's death? he finally asked himself, knowing that he would never ask any of his friends how they reached equanimity.

After Crab Orchard the regiment lay in camp for three days, during which time Jonah's cloudy thinking nearly became opaque; he once again began to feel the debilitating burden of his congealing fear. By the end of the first day, the bite of uncontrollable introspection became intolerable. He fled to church service with renewed dedication and sought the company of new men who seemed enthusiastic for the fight. But the greenhorns' ego-based banter quickly rang hollow. Neither faith in God's will nor the logic of fatalism, a thought process that had saved him at Shiloh, now served to rescue him.

Daunting episodes of ungrounded, unfounded fear, haunting phenomenon laced with hallucinations, began to strike without warning. Fitful sleep plagued him each night, its tossing and turnings laced with recurring nightmares which often stayed with him the following day. In particular, the dream in which he was killed but survived long enough to watch his death would not go away. The dreaded delirium struck three times in one week, high-noon vivid, and he remembered every detail.

On the third night his eyes snapped wide open like exploded kernels of popcorn. Sightless in the pitch-black darkness, he heard only an endless fusillade of raindrops drumming the tent canvas just inches above his flared nose, the relentless pelting keeping him locked rigid. Close. Too close in the tent. Suffocating.

He felt a knot of fear deep in his bowels grow and swell, creeping up his intestines to his heart, where the fear intensified to become razor-sharp terror. He shuddered. Barely breathing, Jonah drew his left hand to his chest and fingered his shirt. Nothing. But it had to be there. It had to. He felt his chest again. Nothing. His shirt was dry. There was no blood. But it had happened. It *did*. It was *real*. He blinked and began to examine the terrifying nightmare he had once again escaped. Be thorough this time, he told himself, look closely. He *must* find something hidden in the episode while it was still fresh, the key, the thing that would make sense of it, render it harmless and make it go away forever. He started at the beginning:

In a solid skirmish line, the Yankees lay elbow-to-elbow staring across the meadow, straight out over its carpet of ankle-high springtime phlox trembling in the breeze. He saw the Rebels coming out of the woods. The enemy seemed to drift toward Jonah in line of battle, three feet apart in perfect order, their muskets riding on their shoulders, their bayonets flashing silver in the bright sunshine. All were dressed in regulation gray uniforms, coming straight at the Union battle line in precise rhythm as if they were a single thing. They were completely silent–no cadence call, no drums, no Rebel yells.

Without signal the entire Union line suddenly rose to its feet, shouldered arms and began parading toward the enemy. Jonah found himself sucked up with them, carried along by the weight of his comrades' overpowering unity. The two neat rows of militia advanced as if the one could not see the other, as if the foe was not there. As the lines closed on each other, Jonah began searching the Rebels' impassive faces.

Like sightless zombies, the soldiers walked through each others' ranks without touching, staring straight ahead, and when the lines reached opposite sides of the trampled meadow, each man spun around and promptly lodged his weapon's butt against his shoulder, aimed, and fired. A large hole ruptured Jonah's chest the instant he shot the man across from him. A black jell began oozing from the cavity. He could see his heart beating inside, but there was no blood. He felt nothing.

He shouldered his musket with the others and marched forward. As the stone-faced men drew together at center-meadow, Jonah could see a gaping rift in each Rebel chest, a milky lard seeped from their wounds. When the Union soldiers gained their original skirmish line, he glanced back to see the Confederates vanishing into the woods behind him; without making a sound, everyone around him wheeled and fell forward into their old prone positions.

Jonah knelt and cautiously pushed his fist into his chest, knowing that he must fill the sucking rupture to make himself whole again. Thick, black blood began to leak down his wrist. He could feel his heart beating. It was then he heard the rain on the canvas above his face.

· · · · ·

For the next two months Jonah tried to escape his torment by focusing on the perfection of the young woman, Molly Reed, who had transfixed him in the barn and at Hickory Creek. Her startlingly clear visage, her jet-black hair and white, flowing dress always comforted him. He often imagined her presence, especially her soft smile–her silent approval brought him peace. Her quiet acceptance of him demanded nothing, only that he exist, unchanged, as he was. Jonah sought Molly's company every day, and when she came to him she was always the embodiment of perfection, and nothing else mattered. He alone had discovered her, and she was his, and he could do with her as he pleased.

But the young woman stayed with him only a few minutes. In spite of Jonah's best efforts, Molly was always followed by the image of Sergeant Vieland's corpse, a white, radiant cross, looming above him. And now the pleasures of Shelbyville seemed long ago, and a new enemy, winter, was closing in. There was no going back.

. . . . .

Relevant Diary Entries

Friday Oct 10th
We marched at 7 A.M. and went up the pike 3 miles and then took off the pike We heard firing off to the right We encamped at 3 P.M. in Walnut grove. It rained on until night

Sat Oct 11th 1862
While we were eating breakfast the rebels attacked our pickets and came up in sight of camp. Our battery threw a few shell at them, and we fell in and marched out and laid in line of battle until 5 P.M.

Sunday Oct 12th 1862
We marched at 8 A.M. We went out across the field and crossed the Danville pike and kept on towards Dick River. We formed a line of battle at 11 and marched about

one mile and halted and laid in line about 2 hours and countermarched about 2 miles and encamped

Mond Oct 13ᵗʰ 1862
We formed a line of battle at 4 A.M. and marched at 8 A.M. We went back on the pike and went down within one mile of Danville I was on guard at headquarters.

Tues Oct 14ᵗʰ
We got orders to march at 1 A.M. The brigade moved out at 1. I staid back with the guard and started at 3 A.M. I stoped at a house and got a good breakfast. The brigade had a skirmish at Stanford I caught up with the Regt at 2 P.M. while they were in line of battle. The rebels fell back and after throwing a few shell we moved on through town and we encamped one mile from Stanford.

Wed Oct 15ᵗʰ 1862
We marched at sunrise There was skirmishing commenced again in front at 8 oclock There was a heavy skirmish at Crab Orchard. We passed through thare at 2 P.M. and at 9 oclock at night

Sat Oct 18ᵗʰ
We started out again this morning to reinforce Gen Vancleve. We passed through Mt Vernon at 11 A.M. We went within 3 miles of Wild Cat and encamped at 2 P.M.

Wed Oct 22ⁿᵈ 1862
Reveille at 4 A.M. and marched at 6 We passed through Mt Vernon at 10 A.M. and encamped 3 miles below Crab Orchard Co C was on picket.

8.

*"Blessed are ye that hunger now: for ye shall be filled.
Blessed are ye that weep now: for ye shall laugh." Luke
6:21*

The clash of the two armies at Perryville resolved nothing. After the bloody encounter, Confederate General Bragg simply continued to maneuver for position, hoping to gain strategic advantage and destroy the enemy, or at least discourage the Federals from moving toward Chattanooga, the high road to the heart of the South. But General Buell's army stayed hot on Bragg's heels. As part of it, the men of Hascall's Brigade moved fast, challenging their supply wagons to keep up with them, which required the 26th Ohio Volunteers to pack heavier than usual and strike out foraging for game and roughage at every opportunity. Rebel raiding parties drew the fractured Army of the Ohio left and right like "stallions after a mare in heat," according to Shoemaker. In mid-October, along with the rest of his company, he was recovering from one of many exhausting scouting treks.

The next day, Company clerk John Ashburn, an

experienced scavenger, mentioned to Elias Cole and Jonah that the Miller farm, located north of Columbia on the Russell River, was becoming known as a cornucopian larder for stray Yankees. Without delay, Jonah asked Sergeant Wicker, the new company first sergeant, if he could lead a three-man foraging party to the Miller farm.

"Probably a waste a time at this late date, corporal," Wicker replied, "but see if he's got any sleepin' straw left. I'll send a wagon if it turns out you need it."

Ten minutes after the foragers stepped onto Miller's front porch, the three hungry soldiers were devouring sweet potatoes and grapes as if there were no tomorrow, giving old man Miller, a widower, second thoughts about the rewards of Christian charity. But tomorrow did come, and so, once again, did the three starved scouts, this time led by Captain Ross and flanked by John Shoemaker and Sam Fry. Invited inside, the six men sat at the kitchen table and bolted down their pork chop and potato suppers like ravenous dogs. They thanked and shook hands with their host on the front porch, and when Miller offered them a sack of corn meal, Shoemaker nearly ran to the barn. He came back grinning, carrying two bags. Captain Ross made him return one, in spite of Miller's objection to his order.

A snowstorm struck in the early hours of Saturday, October 25, piling up six inches in the night and startling the soldiers with its unbroken purity as they crawled from their tents that morning. At first delighted by the white blanket masking the dark, icy woods, the men's spirits rose, but as the day wore on the wind increased and it became bitterly cold. Their morning smiles turned to afternoon frowns.

Feeding their campfires steadily now, the men scrounged for wood and sleeping straw every day, quickly learning that the steady cold of winter, while living a sustained existence in the field, could be profoundly miserable. When their hands seemed to freeze stiff, they shoved them into manure piles to keep the blood moving, but warm dung, as well as the animals that produced it, had become scarce. Horses were now butchered at the first sign of lameness.

Huddling in front of the roaring fire at sundown, Jonah felt the icy breath of darkness rake his backside. He had been on guard duty at brigade headquarters all day, and the body heat he had generated from the walk back to camp had worn off, causing nightfall to seem even colder. Cole and Fry stood across the fire from him, hands extended toward the flames. John Shoemaker came from the latrine and squatted next to him.

"Guess the Rebs won't be runnin' so fast any more," Shoemaker boomed, thrusting his palms toward the glowing coals.

"Froze to death like we be here?" Cole thumped, his unsolicited comment flaring everyone's brows. Shoemaker chuckled.

"That too, Elias. But more likely 'cause they want the war finished quick. I just heard...startin' this month they're all in the scrap for as long as it lasts. Every man-jack is fightin' 'till it's over, now. No enlistment terms no more for the Secesh."

"Glad to hear it," Jonah muttered, "I'm tired a playin' hide-and-seek with the lot. They'll never scatter the buffaloes this'a way." The men glanced at each other, but said nothing. It had grown too cold to talk about things that had nothing to do with finding warmth.

A twelve-wagon train carrying clothes and ammunition, escorted by mounted infantry, caught up with the brigade on October 29. At morning formation the following day, Captain Ross ordered Company C to report to the quartermaster for winter issue. The eighty-four men lined up behind a Conestoga wagon with four hobbled mules in front eating from a trough lashed to the wagon's tongue, supported by a barrel at the far end. The soldiers signed a receipt for their greatcoats, donned them immediately and kept them on all day and night. Knee-length, the coats had capes that fell to the elbow, lined with cloth of the infantry hue.

The supply train also delivered three young recruits. More often than not, fresh troops showed up as formed companies or even regiments, and the arrival of the three surprised Wicker, the new company first sergeant. Only the Confederates, he said, mix stray recruits with veteran outfits now. Sergeant Wicker did not train the new men, but left their education in the hands of the veterans.

The next day, Colonel Fyffe read a general order to his assembled regiment, informing them that General William Rosecrans had relieved General Don Carlos Buell on the 24th. With the 43-year-old General Rosecrans came a new name for his army–The Army of the Cumberland.

"Old Rosie'll give the Secesh hell," Shoemaker declared after dismissal from Fyffe's assembly, "since he don't fritter away chances like some others we know."

The towns flew by: Glasgow on the 31st, Cave City for rations on the first of November, then Scottsville, where General Rosecrans swung his army south into Tennessee, as yet without firing a shot. By the time the 26th arrived at Gallatin, Tennessee, they had outrun their supply wagons once again and were put on half rations. Hungry and tired, the regiment settled into a ten-day camp. Jonah went on official forages every morning during the hiatus, leading a crew from Company C. On one lucky trip they discovered a persimmon grove and carried three gunnysacks full of persimmons back to camp, enough to dull the knives of the entire company.

But, simply scrounging for food did not relieve Jonah's consuming anxiety, or serve to deflect his mental agony as earlier fights had. He longed to meet the enemy as much as General Rosecrans seemed to, and find relief from his living nightmare.

On Tuesday, November 11, the regiment struck out to reinforce the 3rd Ohio Cavalry against John Hunt Morgan's cavalry, but instead of engaging the enemy, they found the 3rd camped on a flat meadow bordering an iced-over creek, relaxing around scattered fires. As the 26th broke from the timber and discovered the idle cavalry, Shoemaker lost control.

"What're they doin', plannin' their hog reconnoiter so's they can have a pig roast afore dark? Damn! Where's Morgan?"

Jonah, desperate for mental diversion and the emotional relief he knew a fight would bring, felt his blood boil at the sight of the cavalry's cookfire smoke and hobbled horses.

Becoming desperate to subdue Morgan's raiders, Rosecrans sent General Wood's entire division, which included the 26th Ohio, east toward Lebanon on the fifteenth to chase Morgan. Early on the second morning, mounted Federal scouts closed in fast on the enemy, racing ahead to fix the Rebels' position. But, although the Federal infantry quicktimed after the scouts for three hours, again the Confederate raider escaped.

Jonah, once more feeling the sting of self-doubt, became desperate. The last thing he wanted to do was talk to someone about his feelings, but he could not help himself. He saw John Shoemaker sitting on a leveled wagon tongue shaving a clump of sassafras roots with his pocketknife. He sat down beside him. They were alone.

"Ya gotta be thirsty to cut sassafras," Jonah muttered, watching him dice the roots into a can of water.

"No coffee for a week...better'in nothin', my friend!"

"You got heated when we found the Third Cav'ry gave up on Morgan, John...you got mad at 'em, didn't you?"

"Damn right."

"How come?"

"I want it ended, don't you?"

Then it just came out.

"Even if your kilt?"

"I ain't gonna get kilt, Jonah."

"You know that for sure?"

"I know that for sure."

"How?"

"I just know it. Don't you?"

Shoemaker stopped slicing his tubers. They looked at each other.

"I think on it now and again, John. How is it you know for certain? You had a sign? You feel somethin'...?"

"I don't feel nothin'. I just know. You feel scared 'bout it?"

"No, not exactly, but I think on it."

"Lookee here, Jonah, you can't let a thing like that cudgel yer brains. Make up yer mind. Like I did."

Shoemaker went back to work and they sat in silence. Jonah stood.

"If you know for certain, how come you're in such a hurry for the end of it?"

"'Cause I don't want no one else kilt, Jonah. No one."

The following day, a sudden, freezing rain turned to ice as it hit the ground, and the men searched for dry straw and firewood like pack rats. As the soldiers sat around the fire that evening, Elias Cole showed Jonah the diary he had started the previous February when the outfit was camped on the Green River in Kentucky. Cole had recorded the distances marched between towns and camps, noting what the weather was like as they went. Elias had traced the 26th Infantry all the way out of Kentucky through Tennessee and into Mississippi, then east through upper Alabama and north through Tennessee and Kentucky again. One thousand six hundred and thirty-four miles. "The tally leaves out the scouts an' reconnoiters," he noted, "which adds considerable to the figger."

"A lot of them miles were ate up at the quicktime an' doublequick, too," Jonah added, handing back the booklet.

"You want to hold the diary for me, Jonah?"

"Why?"

Cole slipped it into his pocket, turned away to stare into the flames and said nothing more. They went to their tents.

Jonah banked straw under his head and drew up his blanket, hoping for a night of untroubled sleep. He closed his eyes but could not relax, remembering the desperation in Cole's eyes. Elias seemed frightened, as if he knew something but could not talk about it. Jonah had decided that he wanted no part of his friend's dilemma. But why not? His comrade, a solid, trusting man, had asked him for a favor, and he had turned him down. Why?

And then he realized why Cole's pleading eyes had frightened him. The man thought he might be killed, *knew it for sure,* maybe, and wanted to leave part of himself behind, in safekeeping with Jonah. An overwhelming compulsion seized Jonah, and like Cole he felt a desperate need to reach out, but there was no one...except Molly Reed. She was the one, the one who understood without any pretensions or worldly affectations, the one who could keep him safe. He tried to picture Molly–it was taking a chance to evoke her image, since she always transmuted to Luke Vieland at the end, then floated above him, a brilliant white cross, a drifting albino hawk looking down to destroy Jonah's refuge.

He would write Molly a letter tomorrow, and it would explain everything. And then someone else would know his feelings, but understand him this time. How would it start? Like any other letter he had written to his family, simply....

...Dear Miss Molly Reed:

My friend, Jas. Bradfield, is headed by wagon to his uncle's place at Flat Creek to heal a leg he broke on a fall that splintered it, and since your farm is on the way, Jas. said he would deliver my writing to you.

We never had time to discuss much about ourselves, but I think of you often, and specially that morning at Hickory Creek. It meant a lot to me over the months. In this here letter I will try to explain my life, praying that you find my effort of interest.

I was born at Delaware County Ohio in 1843, and even then our folks were riled about the ways of the Southern folks, knowing trouble was coming. Ever since I was old enough to listen, I heard people speak of The Great Cause, and how it would set things straight.

Long before Fort Sumpter Pa said a civil war was coming and we would soon amputate a few of the countrys putrefying limbs in order to stop the infection spread. I reached army age and went straightaway to Ashley and enlisted, knowing God's will was behind all us Ohio boys who stepped forward.

We were a force for righteousness, the final cure for the immoral disease of secession, and we were obliged to put the nation back on its rightful path. Everyone called it The Great Cause. The men who could took up arms for the glory of God, but a few stubborn mules would not stand for the harness, and they can be damned.

I recall the great cyclone storm of '59 when Reverend Sable preached about Divine intervention, how the evil ways of some men could not be tolerated, and that they had made the cyclone storm necessary. Lightning had torched off our barn, and Pa, thinkin he might be among the evil that caused it, blamed himself. And that is what happened to the whole country, going up in flames like the barn, but we know now that the Southern sinners caused God to have a war to settle it, not us. Anyways, from then on it was a scarce Sunday when The Great Cause was not spoke at Reverend Sables pulpit.

Now and then the preacher called Weld's Apostles up from Columbus, and the Apostles always got to the point real quick. Weld's men knew the history of it, too, and once told us about Episcopal Bishop Hopkins in Vermont throwing out brothers who spoke for abolition, but the Apostles said that those days are gone forever, and that wont happen no more in the church, especially in Ohio. I hung on every word, and afterwards I listened to the grownups discussing the subject like they had figgured the whole thing out thereselves. Everyone wanted to be a part of The Great Cause.

As I lay here in my tent tonight, Molly, I hear a winter storm coming, and the roll and rumble reminds me of Reverend Sable's words thundering out. He was a measured man, turning his head slow side-to-side, calculating as he spoke, and thumping his fist every time he said God.

He would stare at the ceiling after he spoke, letting his words sink into us, and everyone looked at him, thinking about what he just said, froze in our pews, even the children. Then he went on, starting slowly and picking up speed like the railroad cars, and sometimes I swore I saw white smoke puffing out of his head, just like the engine, and the glint from his glasses, and his black hair flashing at me. The reverend made everything clear for me, black and white clear.

I do my best every day in the army, Molly, avoiding sinful ways like I was taught, and keeping clean, but lately I been troubled. Remembering our Maker helps me sometimes, but from day to day the war seems more and more like chasing lice…there aint no end to it. I worry I wont see you again, wont see anybody for that matter. It's not that I am scared exactly, but that maybe God, well, not exactly God, but something will cause things to go wrong, and I wont have the strength to face it. So I think about you, and then I can go on, and then, well, sometimes you dont come to me Molly, and then…and then….

…Tears welled in Jonah's eyes, and he squeezed them. He lay quietly, even though his chest felt as if it would explode. An hour later his mind finally collapsed and he drifted asleep.

· · · · ·

The regiment settled into winter camp just east of Nashville at the end of November, and on the second of December marched in a Grand Review for Colonel Wilder. The colonel sat his black stallion ramrod straight, a clean-cut, determined figure in regulation uniform, inspiring all who could see him.

Colonel Wilder had surrendered to the Rebels the previous September, overpowered at Mumfordsville by General Bragg's main force. Outnumbered ten to one and with no relief possible, he had managed to get good surrender terms by bluffing Bragg into believing that he was part of a larger force. And now, the men who had chased Bragg out of Mumfordsville hoping to avenge the colonel's defeat, marched with renewed energy, impressed by Wilder's soldiering skills and his ability to get paroled by the enemy.

Another Grand Review was held on Thursday the fourth for their new commander, Major General "Rosie" Rosecrans, and after the parade, C Company gathered at the sutler's tent. It was payday.

"Old Rosie looked a mite pale," Shoemaker pointed out while standing in line at the taffy counter, which consisted of a plank resting on two barrels.

"Almost white as the mare he set on," Fry added.

"Thar weren't much of a rose look 'bout him. Whar's the 'Rosie' come from?" asked Ashburn, the company clerk.

Captain Ross brushed past carrying a new, boxed derringer. He stopped and looked back. "The nose, men, you didn't see the nose? But let me tell you something—that glowing nose can smell a Rebel ten miles downwind." Having seen no Rebels, the men remained unconvinced of the general's olfactory sensitivity, but smiled politely.

And for nearly a month after Captain Ross' comment at the confection counter, the army went nowhere, a victim, apparently, of confusing scents on the wind.

During the December hiatus, the brigade held four turkey shoots. In addition, regimental knife-throwing matches took place after each Saturday parade, the contests rumored to be part of Colonel Fyffe's program to have fun while honing fighting skills. Moving back three paces after hitting the mark dead center, Jonah was most often the last man to stick the target, winning three out of four matches. Captain Ross donated a black, leather-bound Bible for one of the prizes, from which Jonah read the Scriptures daily.

On Friday, the fifth of December, freezing air pressed the men all day, and that evening a sleet storm drove wildly through their camp, followed by a heavy snowstorm starting just after midnight. When the wind finally died at dawn, the woods lay covered with a soft white blanket of snow, but the purified landscape went unnoticed in the gut-numbing cold. The roads had become frozen, iron-hard ruts.

In spite of the pervasive cold weather, Company C warmed slightly on December 11 during a minor clash with the enemy. The company, called out just before sundown to guard a forage train on its last leg into camp, was ambushed on a thickly wooded bend in the road, a curve that hid nearly everything ahead of them. Rebel skirmishers, sneaking up on the Federals, immediately drove in the train's outriders, and C Company, flanking the wagons at the bend in the road, quickly condensed into a line of battle, taking cover in a drainage ditch opposite the Rebels. The caravan raced ahead. Three Rebels were killed and a dozen were thought to be shot, but no Yankees were seriously hurt in the scrap.

As the men reformed on the road, preparing to march, Jonah suddenly realized that he had once again escaped himself during the melee. He tried to relive the event as they marched route-step down the road, but simply thinking about it was not the same. Huddled around the fire that evening, the men recounted the event, but their spirited banter left him undistracted and indifferent. Fry changed the subject.

"I seen orders on the division board puttin' Colonel Fyffe in charge of a whole brigade," he announced, staring into the flames. Jonah remembered when the colonel, sick as a dog, stayed behind at the National hotel in Louisville while Captain Hicks led his recruits, bursting with enthusiasm, to the regiment last February, nearly a year ago. The journey seemed long ago and far away, an indistinct, colorless shadow buried in the past.

"I asked Captain Ross if he found out from the surgeon yet what kilt Sergeant Vieland," Shoemaker rumbled as if he had not heard Fry, "but he said he still don't know a thing. Two nights ago I suffered a dream with the sergeant in it," he added. The men stared into the flames. No one spoke.

But Jonah knew about nightmares, and, shuddering, he recalled his latest one. Trapped in a tar pit with black pitch gripping his chest, he looked up to see Vieland kneeling on the edge above. The sergeant reached down and he reached up, but he could not quite get a grip on his savior's hand, and the tar kept getting hotter. He awoke with a start. It was as if he had died and was being sucked down into hell, and the sergeant still lived and wanted him back. But the hell of the dream could be no worse than the living hell he now suffered.

Just before taps that evening, Jonah borrowed a candle from Sam Fry, slid his black leather Bible from his pack and fanned it open. The pages splayed, and he looked down to see 1 Corinthians, chapter 1, verse 19. His lips moved as he read:

> For it is written, I will destroy the wisdom of the
> wise, and will bring to nothing the understanding
> of the prudent.

Jonah blew out the candle and stared into the darkness, listening to the bugler's mournful roundelay.

. . . . .

Relevant Diary Entries

Sat Oct 25th
We marched at 7 It was a cold cloudy day It rained some in the afternoon, and froze as it fell. We encamped at 5 P.M. one mile from Columbia. There was six inches of snow fell in the night

Sun Oct 26th
It was a cold morning Jess Mason, Jon Ashburn and I went out foreging. We got our dinners and some sweet potatoes at Mr Millers, and went back to camp

Mond Oct 27th 1862
It was a clear warm day John Ashburn and I went out to Millers again after our dinners.

Tues Oct 28th
Capt Ross Elias Cole, Jno Hall and I went out again and got our dinners.

Wed Oct 29th 1862
S.G. Fry, Simpson, Mason and I went out and got our dinners. Our tents and baggage came up this A.M. and our recruits joined the Regt

Sat Nov 1st 1862
The division moved at daylight. The 26th and 100th Ill was rear guard behind the train. We got to camp at 7 A.M. Co C and 3 other companies of the 26th went with a train to Cave City after grub. We got there at 7 P.M.

Wed Nov 5th
We marched at 7 A.M. and encamped at dark at Scottsville We pitched our tents at 9 P.M. it rained some through the night

Sat Nov 8th
We marched at 6 A.M. and passed through Gallatin at 11 ½ A.M. We encamped 3 miles south of town. Jno Hall and I went out foreging We were on half rations

Tues Nov 11th
We drew rations in the A.M. and we got orders to march at 2 P.M. immediately. We were ready in five minutes. We went out to reinforce the 3rd Ohio cavalry who was out on a hog reconnoiter, with Morgans cavalry. We went out 11 miles and then cameback to camp where we arrived at 10 P.M.

Wed Nov 26th
We struck tents at 10 A.M. and marched at 12 M. We went very slow until we crossed Mill creek, at 4 P.M. We left the Lebanon pike, and came across the country, and encamped on the Nashville and Chatanooga R.R. at 8 P.M.

Sund Nov 30
Our Regt went out foreging with a large wagon train We went out 6 miles and got back to camp at 3 P.M. rainy in the P.M.

Tues Dec 2nd
We had grand review by Col Wylder at 2 P.M. and then had battalion drill

Wed Dec 3rd 1862
Capt Ross, Capt Besto J.B. Richardson, John Black, and I went Nashville

Thurs Dec 4th
We had grand review by Maj Gen Rosecrans. We at 11 A.M. and came to camp at 3 P.M.

Frid Dec 5th
There was quite a heavy snow storm in the A.M. it froze pretty hard in the night

Thurs Dec 11th
Our brigade went out with a forage train. We drove in the rebel pickets and skirmished with them until sundown and then camp back to camp.

Christmas 1862
We – the 26 – went out foreging and got back at 9 P.M. after a march of 25 miles

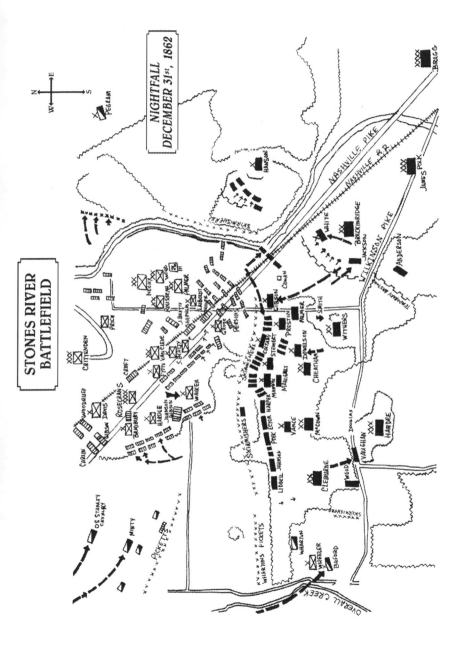

9.

"For it is written, I will destroy the wisdom of the wise, and will bring to nothing the understanding of the prudent." 1 Corinthians 1:19

At 7:30 a.m. on Friday, December 26, 1862, the 26th Ohio Volunteers left their bivouac in a muddy cow pasture one mile west of Martha, Tennessee, and headed south toward Murfreesboro, straight into the jaws of the monster from hell. As part of the fully provisioned and well-organized Army of the Cumberland, they moved quickly, having wagoned their unessential baggage and trappings back to Nashville, as had the other regiments. The battalion commanders deployed skirmishers as soon as they struck out; the 26th heard heavy firing close in front before the regiment had gone ten miles. With some trepidation, the soldiers followed in the wake of the sporadic cacophony throughout the day.

At 10 a.m. the next morning they fixed bayonets and charged through a well-defended village called La Verne, where eighteen men from the regiment were seriously wounded, including Tom Shotwell from Company C. The soldiers were not allowed fires that evening, but ate their cold rations with gusto.

"Whut the hell we got up front," Shoemaker asked, slapping a hardtack biscuit against his musket stock, "the whole keeboodle? They ain't runnin' too quick this time."

"Not so's you'd notice," Fry mumbled.

"Bragg's got Breckenridge with him, ain't you heerd?" Cole said, snatching up a chunk of Shoemaker's broken biscuit that had fallen to the ground.

Attendance swelled at church the following day, Sunday, reflecting the men's rising apprehension. Services were held in the open in brilliant morning sunshine, a welcome warming. Jonah also went to the second service at noon, but by then gray clouds stretched from horizon to horizon.

Beginning at first light on Monday, the 29th, the Army of the Cumberland, in a carefully coordinated advance, drove the Rebels to within 3 miles of Murfreesboro, where the 26th camped along the Nashville railroad tracks at nightfall. Unknown to Jonah and his comrades, the two massed armies were about to fight one of the most wrenching struggles of the Civil War—*The Battle of Stones River*, afterward referred to as *The Battle of Murfreesboro* by the Southerners.

After a year of fragmented, poorly coordinated fighting, the Federal as well as the Confederate army was anchored by seasoned soldiers eager to vent pent-up aggression, men ready to hunker down with a determination not seen since Shiloh Church. The impending conflagration at Stones River would be an awakening for both General Rosecrans and General Bragg, a chilling, on-the-job lesson that would teach them not to underestimate the enemy's willingness to absorb an onslaught and still fight despite stunning blows.

Unlike the testy probings and brief skirmishes of the past summer, the combatants would clash headlong in a fierce, three-day brawl that would kill nearly 3,000 outright and bloody over 15,000. Most of the crippled men would soon die from their wounds.

. . . . .

The feeble December sun had reached its winter solstice, hovering low over the still battleground, gathering energy for its annual transcendent journey north. Winter's brief days fell swiftly to long, cold nights; the quiet killing fields lay bleak, their fallow earth and leafless trees indifferent to man's cataclysmic struggle with himself. Nature had set her most dismal stage for the darkest drama in the human repertoire.

The Ohio volunteers were called into line of battle at 5 a.m. on Wednesday the thirty-first, the final gasp of 1862. The turbid darkness hid regiments from each other; only the occasional sound of clanking gear or a shouted command reassured the men that they were a part of a larger force.

Suddenly cannon blasts and sharp musketry exploded close on the right of the Ohio men, close enough for them to feel the hot concussions–they hit the ground, stunned, knowing for certain that they would get an order to charge. But they did not. Instead, they lay until first light, listening to the rip of musket volleys and the thunder of cannon dead ahead and on the right. Then General Wood's entire division, the 26th in the vanguard, threw itself into the chaos on the Union right flank, and as Wood's Division charged, his surging regiments collided with the bloodied men of retreating Union Generals Johnson and Davis.

Jonah dashed forward, up a wooded hillside, his breath came in gasps, he could not feel his legs moving. Cold air teared his eyes, nearly blinding him. Suddenly a blow slammed his stomach and he staggered backward then fell, his rump cushioned by his haversack. Rolling sideways to his knees, he clutched his stomach. In front of him lay his musket, its stock smashed by a Rebel ball. He sprang to his feet and raced ahead, snatching up a lost weapon as he ran.

The tough Ohio veterans, undeterred by the chaos surrounding them, pressed forward, finally coming into the open, face-to-face with the enemy. Their lines solidified as they paused to fire with greater accuracy, kneeling to reload and rising to fire again. They took cover and held their ground, repulsing three tenacious Confederate counterattacks. When the Rebels finally withdrew, Wood's Division fell back for ammunition, replaced by Fyffe and Beatty's brigades.

"God damn," Goodhue mumbled, strapping on his loaded cartridge box then glancing at his pocket watch, "hit's jest two o'clock."

Nearly exhausted but replenished, the 26th immediately bolted left at the doublequick to support one of Colonel Wagner's exposed artillery batteries. After they lunged into position they found themselves trapped in a scorching Rebel artillery crossfire. Refusing to retreat, the regiment began to suffer losses from the well-positioned Confederate batteries. Once the Confederate batteries were silenced and Wagner's Union battery seemed secure, companies A and C were pulled out under rifle fire to save an 8th Indiana artillery battery from being captured by advancing enemy infantry.

The two Ohio companies took position in front of the battery, repulsing a charge, but before another charge could be mounted, the sinking sun began to plunge the smoke-laced battlefield into darkness. Lingering Confederate units started to slowly fall back, and as they did the steady roar of battle gradually lapsed to intermittent sniping. The men lay without shelter or fires where nightfall struck them, their surging adrenaline finally overcome by physical exhaustion.

Wood's Division had sustained crippling losses, but Captain Ross' casualty report for Company C listed only four relatively minor woundings. The three recruits that First Sergeant Wicker had not trained, Jonathan Sherwood, Aaron Brown and Charles Martin, were among the wounded. Sherwood died an hour later from what at first appeared to be a superficial head wound.

Bragg's Generals Hardee and Polk had delivered the most severe and prolonged onslaught, a bloody drubbing by any measure, which Jonah Hommen and his fellow Union soldiers, excluding the Shiloh veterans, had yet endured. At the onset, the Confederates had hurled themselves into the Federal right flank, driving it back with a sustained determination unimagined by the Northern troops, who had been lulled into false confidence by months of crafty Rebel hit-and-run tactics. But it was not over.

Jonah crawled to a shallow swale behind a stand of splintered poplar trees. The trees' shot-away limbs lay helter-skelter in front of him like matchsticks dumped from a box. His numb legs, seemingly disconnected and beyond control, began to quiver in spastic cycles, taking on a life of their own. Suddenly his right leg began to convulse like a bludgeoned animal senselessly struggling to escape an already delivered deathblow. The convulsion ended and he finally lay still, staring into the black night, listening to the groans of the wounded and the clank of lost equipment being gathered. A trace chain rattled behind him and he looked back; out of the darkness came a wagon loaded with bodies, nearly running over him as it creaked toward the Nashville Pike.

In bizarre contrast with the battle's fury, military bands from both sides struck up in competition, their echoic strains wafting over the one-mile front with nightmarish absurdity. *Camptown Races* broke the stillness, its distant tones rising and falling in the still night air. *The Battle*

Hymn of the Republic drifted from far to the rear, and *My Old Kentucky Home* washed over Jonah from close ahead, drowning out the Yankee hymn. As the music pulsed over him, he pictured the Confederate musicians playing Foster's song, suddenly remembering the Rebel soldier he had seen when they raced to save the 8th Indiana battery...

...only twenty yards in front of him, Jonah watched the young Rebel stand up and turn to run, but at that instant a cannon ball struck the soldier's neck, and his head fell backward to his shoulder blades and stayed there, held by a strip of skin, and before his body fell, the young Rebel stared upside down at him, and now Jonah heard *My Old Kentucky Home* and squeezed his eyes and saw the Rebel's upside-down face, and the music kept playing, and he thought he might also like to die quickly now.

The temperature continued to drop; the chilling air tightened its grip. Jonah's body began to shiver in cycles, its fitful quavering gradually warping into rhythmic tremors. His trembling, at first the product of nervous exhaustion, became worse as his icy, sweat-wet clothing began to stick to his cooling skin. A moan escaped his powder-blackened lips as he watched frost crystals form along his glinting musket barrel and coat sleeves. His neck told him that his woolen cape had grown dew-wet in the damp air, and he looked around to see it slowly freezing into a carpet of ice crystals. His breath stabbed white, gossamer plumes into the blackness, the vapor drifting up to disappear into the gray gun smoke layered above him. At last his eyelids began to drift closed, his jaw nudged his shoulder and slushy sputum dribbled from the corner of his mouth into his cape's crystals, the slaver slowly etching a path through the clinging rime.

In a desperate attempt to sleep, he tried to capture the image of Molly in the barn doorway, then as she lifted her pale face from the pooled water at Hickory Creek. Try as he might, he found he could no longer invoke her presence. His pulsing mind began to collapse from the weight of his mental effort. A warming numbness, a feathery lightness spread through his spent muscles. The sense that he had been abandoned, deserted by God and man, struck him, and he lay in a semi-conscious trance.

Suddenly, from far away, a resonant voice blinked his eyes. The battlefield vanished. In front of him appeared his father, mother and sister sitting with him in a church pew. Reverend Sable's explosive timbre swelled from the pulpit. Jonah could not escape it:

"The world *need not be chaotic!*" The preacher slowly raised his fist. Jonah winced. "God (thump!) has a plan for his children! God (thump!) has a plan for our nation and every walkin', crawlin', flyin' creature in it! The sacred Bible and our Declaration of Independence come from *above, Divinely inspired!*" he bellowed, pointing toward the beamed ceiling, "and to ignore these writs is to go against *God* (thump!). We must choose our direction...free will is a Divine blessin'. So, Jonah, are *you* walkin' God's (thump!) path? *"Are you?"*

. . . . .

At 3 a.m. on New Year's Day, the Ohio troops were again deployed to the right flank, but as soon as they arrived they were ordered to quicktime back to the front they had just left. Jonah hit the ground with Fry on his right and Cole on his left. Shoemaker crawled over on his hands and knees, collapsing to his stomach alongside Fry. The silent darkness seemed to hammer them—no one said a word. A sense of unity and safety washed over Jonah as he lay among his friends, and he slept for over an hour. At first light the men formed ranks and marched one mile to a reserve area along the Nashville railroad tracks.

Generals Rosecrans and Bragg, it seemed, needed time to think things over. Guessing each other's vulnerabilities, they began to consolidate and reposition their forces, each trying to find the key that would snap open the slaughterhouse gate and deliver enemy muscle to his grinder. Only skirmishers, positioned less than two hundred yards in front of each other, exchanged fire on the first day of 1863.

At sundown, Hascall's brigade of Wood's division, the 26th leading, moved forward to the battle line, throwing themselves into entrenchments hastily dug by others the previous day. They found themselves at left-center stage. Lying on their backs, the men squeezed together in search of body heat while watching daylight disappear. They lay elbow-to-elbow and motionless, except now and then when someone stirred to eat cold rations.

"Don't look like nobody's runnin' this time," Shoemaker rasped.

"Not so's you'd notice," Fry answered.

"Yep, not so long's thar's any breathin' in the Yankee carcass," someone down the line added.

Jonah heard the words coming from the men, but the noise made no sense, simply rat scratchings in the attic, the vexing sounds of harmless creatures, palaver that meant nothing to him. He felt himself becoming mentally disconnected as a drifting sensation crept over him. The regiment remained on the battle line throughout the night, but few slept for more than an hour at a time.

At first light Jonah realized that he was once again focused. He raised his head enough to see that he was on a slight rise overlooking the Stones River ford, just north of the Nashville Pike. As a few others began to raise themselves, a furious Rebel artillery barrage exploded on their left, driving Union cannoneers and horses from their batteries. They watched in horror as the intense bombardment killed and wounded hundreds of Federals. Then the men lay listening to the sweep of musketry left and right, but no Rebels challenged their position until just after noon.

Shortly before they were attacked, they watched a mass of Confederates consolidate into an offensive formation across the river and shift to their right, then plunge forward through the water to strike the Union left flank. The weight of the attack hammered back Beatty's division, including Colonel Fyffe's brigade. Then the onslaught launched itself at the 26th. Jonah fired into them, but they kept coming. Captain Ross galloped past behind him ordering his men back up a slight rise into shallow entrenchments dug the day before. The 26th retreated fifty yards, hurling itself into the new defensive line, but the enemy pressed forward into their sustained volley, and Jonah kept firing until Federal reinforcements finally swept into the lateral trenches alongside the 26th. The new line held. From their elevated firing position, they were able to drive the Confederates back into a sprawling stand of shot-up trees one hundred yards beyond the open battleground.

In an instant the chaotic roar fell away to nothing. Gasping for breath, the Ohio soldiers lay peering over felled tree trunks fronting their entrenchments, hunting for Rebel stragglers. A cold drizzle, almost sleet, began to fall steadily, but the heated Yankees, jammed shoulder-to-shoulder, could not feel its numbing chill. Powerful, white steam feathers spewed in nervous bursts from their mouths and noses, signaling a temperature plunge; their sweat-soaked greatcoats began to freeze and stiffen.

Sucking deep breaths, Jonah lay clutching his loaded weapon while searching the trees beyond, but he could see no enemy. Then a faint moan came from the trampled muck in front of him, and twenty yards away he saw a man struggling to crawl over the black mud using only his left arm, the other trailing at his side, limp. The soldier's cap and musket were missing, his greatcoat torn away at the waist, and his skewed legs twisted grotesquely with each thrust. The man stopped and slowly lifted his face, blinking into the drizzle. His powder-darkened lips quivered as his eyes searched left and right, and then he reached out with his good arm, sinking his clawed hand into the mire, and pulled. A screaming Minié ball suddenly tore into his back, and Jonah heard the muffled pop of bone snapping under muscled flesh. The man's muddy hand shot to his throat and seemed to prop up his head. He lay motionless with his head propped up, his black lips locked in a frozen grimace. Jonah came alive and started over the logs, but iron fingers gripped his boot. He glanced back.

"It's no use, Jonah, he's dead. Get down."

Jonah collapsed backward against Elias Cole's planted knees.

They stared at the dead soldier lying in front of them, his chin resting on the palm of his crusted hand, sightless eyes wide open, and they watched his face grow ashen then turn white as the freezing rain cleansed his skin. Captain Ross lurched past behind them, sword in hand, ordering his men to shift one hundred yards left. Elias Cole and Jonah were the last to leave.

At four o'clock the second major attack began, and as soon as it did, John Goodhue, the company clerk, stood up and started walking away, back toward the Nashville Pike. Jonah watched Goodhue fling down his musket just as a Rebel shell screamed over his head, landing twenty feet behind Goodhue, skipping into him and blowing him apart. Overwhelming anger filled Jonah, rising above everything else, sweeping away the thunder surrounding him, and he once more saw Goodhue's face looking at his watch when they fell back for ammunition, and he heard his words: "*God damn, hit's jest two o'clock. God damn, hit's jest...God damn...."*

The 26ᵗʰ Ohio held against the determined and resourceful Confederates, who had skillfully combined cannon and infantry in yet another thrust against the Union left flank. But in spite of four devastating attacks, the Federals held. During the final assault, an hour before nightfall, Jonah knew for the first time, and with absolute certainty, that he had killed another human.

Lying in a shallow trench on the crest of a slight rise above Stones River, he could see flat rock outcroppings seventy-five yards in front, natural flagstones descending to the water's edge. Wondering if his feet would ever touch them, he lay on his stomach, set and ready, reloaded and waiting for yet another onslaught. Through the leafless trees on the far riverbank he glimpsed swarms of clustered shadows beginning to emerge from the timber just beyond the river.

The advancing Confederates, uniformly clad in gray, shuffled forward in tight knots, weapons held high as they accelerated toward the waist-deep water at the open ford. Captain Ross dismounted behind his company and drew his sword: *"Get ready men! Hold your fire!"* Jonah steadied in the prone firing position, fixing on a bearded Rebel wearing a gray-caped coat and broad campaign hat. He watched the man bolt toward the water, punching his knees up, musket held high over his head. Jonah aimed dead-center stomach just as Colonel Haskell's sword dropped and Captain Ross shouted *"Fire!"*

Thunder from a thousand muskets belched into Jonah, but he did not shoot. The discharging weapons sent a curtain of smoke leaping forward, at first hiding the enemy, and then it hesitated and began drifting back toward the ensconced infantry, slowly rising above them. The steady rattle of deliberate firing began to cleave the air. Jonah followed his man with his musket barrel, watching him gain the knee-deep water at the ford. He squeezed and the Rebel reeled backward, splashing spread-eagle into the churning shallows. In one swift motion Jonah rolled to his back, reloaded and spun to his elbows, thrusting the musket into his shoulder. He saw the dead man floating face up in the frothy river, a hatless gray cross, his belly clothing clawed open, mouth gaping.

Shortly after sundown, Hascall's Brigade of Wood's Division cautiously forded Stones River in the wake of a final Union counterattack, and Jonah paused at the spot where the charging Rebel fell. But the man lay somewhere downstream now, and only Jonah would ever know who killed him.

. . . . .

A soft, warming sprinkle fell all the next day and night, but the mollifying rain held a bitter heaviness for Jonah. Even his friends' spirited banter, the victory rush, rang hollow in his ears. Keeping to himself, he felt no jubilation.

On picket duty in the early evening of January 3, he sat alone in a bushy copse under his tented rubber blanket, watching distant Rebel campfires flicker through the splintered trees. He drew up his legs and locked his arms around them, then rested his chin on his muddied knees. Watching the steady drizzle wash the black, sticky mire from his boots, he closed his eyes, and the image of the dead infantryman in the water loomed before him. The vision radiated soft light, delicate effulgence appearing around it. He squeezed his eyelids tight and tears came, but the tears did not blur the splayed Rebel corpse.

Suddenly the man he had killed floated toward him and transformed to Sergeant Vieland, lying on his back, a white cross, and then the image quickly disappeared. It

David Jardine

had been three months since Luke Vieland died, but as Jonah sat quietly he felt his presence again. With Vieland's presence came the fleeting embrace of compassionate trust, and then the sergeant's granite self-confidence, the thing Jonah had searched his own viscera to find, touched him for an instant. But the feeling quickly blew away into the cold, wet darkness like steam escaping from under a boiling kettle's cover. He simply stared through the trees at the enemy fires, his mind empty.

· · · · ·

The critical low point of the winter solstice had passed, and the sun once again began spiraling northward from the Tropic of Capricorn, seeking its Vernal Equinox, and when it climbed further to trace the equator, gentle summer days would follow. With summer would come nature's plenty, and unknown to Jonah Hommen, a new beginning.

In the wake of *The Battle of Stones River,* Jonah slowly woke to his growing distrust of social convention, including, what was for him the uncomfortable reliance on the ideas of others, both military and civilian. Trying to live as others would have him live had become a suffocating parody engendered by those who would have everyone cutting by another's plumb. His instinctive reliance on others quietly crumbled and drifted away, overpowered by a personal freedom born of self-awareness. But it would take Chickamauga to wrench up lasting fulfillment, gratitude for simply being alive and whole. Now his mind began to whisper in soft harmony with his spirit–the clear melody would follow.

· · · · ·

138

Fri Dec 26th 1862
We got orders to march at 7 1/2 A.M. Our baggage was sent to Nashville and we started for Murfreesboro there was heavy firing in front all day. We encamped ½ mile from Lavergne

Sat Dec 27th 1862
We fell in at 10 A.M. and marched out before Lavergne, and by order of Gen Haskell fixed bayonet and charged through the town There was 18 wounded from our Regt Billy Wade from Co C. We moved in line of battle and encamped 6 miles

Mond Dec 29th
We were releaved at 10 A.M. and started on the march. We drove the rebels within 3 miles of Murfreesboro and encamped at dark. Had nothing to eat.

Tues Dec 30th
We laid in camp there was heavy fighting all day on the right

Wed Dec 31st 1862
We were called up at 5 A.M. put on our equipment and got our breakfast and remained under arms. There was heavy fireing commenced on the right at sunrise, and Johnsons division was driven back, and our division was ordered out to support the center at 8 oclock We were changing position until 10 oclock when the center fell back and we were drawn into a regular engagement. We repulsed three attacks from the enemy and was then releaved at 2 P.M. and fell back for ammunition. We were then called on to support one of Col Wagoners batteries, to repulse a charge.

We were placed between a heavy cross fire of two of the rebels batteries, killing a number and wounded several of our Regt. We remained there until nearly sundown and then was sent to support the 8th Ind battery where we laid until the firing ceaced for the day. We layed out all night without blankets or fire. We suffered considerable from cold The wounded of our Co was John Ashburn, Jonathan Sherwood, Aaron Brown and Charles Martin

Thurs Jan 1st 1863
We changed position at 3 A.M. and fell back to the rear on reserve and layed there until 9 P.M. and was again sent out in front.

Fri Jan 2nd 1863
There was a skirmish took place at sunrise when our batteries opened on the rebels which was returned with awful fury. The drove horses and men from our batteries killing and wounding quite a number. John Goodhue of our Co was killed by a rebel shell. We held our position all day. There was a hard fight took place across the river. Our men came out victorious, driving everything before them and killed, wounded and captured a large number of rebels. Our division was sent across the river after dark.

Sat Jan 3rd 1863
Our brigade went out on picket at 8 A.M. It rained all day and night. The rebels attacted the center after dark and was driven back by Gen Rosscans division

Sun Jan 4th 63
We crossed the river at 2 A.M. and went up on the R.R. and encamped at daylight. We heard of the Evacuation of Murfreesboro this forenoon.

. . . . .

*Brigadier General Milo Hascall's Report of the Advance to
Stones River*

(Official Record Vol XX, Series 1, Part 1, page 57)

HDQRS, FIRST BRIGADE, FIRST DIVISION, LEFT WING,
Stewart's Creek, Ten., December 28, 1862

...Before we had been five minutes in motion, a brisk fire
was opened by the enemy in and about town [La Vergne]
upon our skirmishers, which soon became effectual upon
the first line also. The fire was vigorously returned by our
skirmisher but, I presume, with little effect, owing to the
cover the town, fences and bushes afforded the enemy.
Not wishing to try and cope with the enemy under such
unfavorable circumstances any longer than was absolutely
necessary, I ordered the skirmishers and the first line to
charge at a double-quick and get possession of the town at
all hazards. The front line was lying flat on their faces at
the time of receiving the order; but in the twinkling of an
eye the entire line sprang to their feet, fixed their bayonets,
and, rushing forward with a yell, had, in five minutes' time,
possession of the town and the crest beyond. The manner in
which this was done left nothing to be desired. Our entire
loss, though skirmishing all day, was sustained at this point.
Twenty of the Twenty-sixth Ohio and 7 of the Fifty-eighth
Indiana were lying around with wounds of greater or less
severity to tell the tale....

...All my officers and men did their duty nobly, and I feel
that it would be unjust to particularize. How much credit
we deserve, I leave for yourself and others to determine....

MILO S. HASCALL
Brigadier-General of Vols.,
Comdg First Division, Left Wing

. . . . .

*Major William H. Squires' Report of the Battle at La Vergne,
Tennessee*

HDQRS. TWENTY-SIXTH OHIO VOLUNTEER INFANTRY,

In Field, near La Vergne, December 28, 1862

SIR: I have the honor to report the following as the part performed by the Twenty-sixth Ohio Volunteer Infantry, under my command, on the 27th instant:

Between 11 and 12 o'clock I first received orders to form the regiment in line of battle, and deploy my flanking companies as skirmishers. This being executed, and the order to advance being given, my skirmishers were ordered to enter La Vergne at a double-quick. On reaching the edge of the town, the firing on them became very severe, and at this point I received the order to advance my regiment at a double-quick and clear the town. This was performed by the regiment to my entire satisfaction. Having passed the town, the regiment, owing to the dense woods and the difficulty of seeing our proper position, obliqued too far to the left, and a part of it was thrown on the left of the railroad, and encountered considerable opposition from a force of the enemy's cavalry, which were finally driven forward. After dispersing this body of cavalry, I received orders to move over to turnpike, which I did, and was there relieved by the One hundredth Illinois Volunteers, which I was then ordered to support....

I regret to report the following loss of enlisted men in my regiment, nearly all of which occurred during the execution of the order to charge through the town, viz: Company A, 1 man wounded; Company B, 2 wounded; Company C, 1 wounded; Company D, 2 wounded; Company F, 1 killed and 2 wounded; Company H, 4 wounded; Company I, 3 wounded; Company K, 2 wounded; total, 17 wounded and 1 killed. In considering the circumstances under which the regiment went into the engagement, to wit, with but 1 acting field officer, 1 acting staff officer, 11 commissioned line officers, and 380 men, under arms, and the fact of the men being heavily laden, their clothes and contents of knapsacks being very wet, I have every reason to be satisfied with their conduct....

My company officers deserve my most sincere thanks for their efforts and the success attained in keeping the men well in hand and perfectly cool.

I have the honor to be, yours, very respectfully,

W. H. SQUIRES,
Commanding Twenty-sixth Ohio Volunteer Infantry.

. . . . .

Brigadier General Milo Hascall's Report of the Battle at Stones River

(Official Record Vol XX, Series 1, Part 1)

HDQRS. FIRST BRIGADE, FIRST DIVISION, LEFT

David Jardine

WING,
Near Murfreesborough January 6, 1863.

SIR: I have the honor to submit the following report of the operations of my brigade (formerly the Fifteenth Brigade, Sixth Division, but under the new nomenclature, the First Brigade, First Division, left wing) on the eventful 31st of December, 1862:

During the night of the 30th, I had received notice, through General Wood, our division commander, that the left wing (Crittenden's corps) would cross Stone's River and attack the enemy on his right. My brigade was posted on the extreme left of our entire line of battle, and was guarding and overlooking the ford, over which we were to cross. On the morning of the 31st, heavy firing was heard on the extreme right of our line (McCooks's corps), but as they had been fighting their way all the distance from Nolensville, as we had from La Vergne, no particular importance was attached to this, and I was getting my brigade into position ready to cross as soon as General Van Cleve's division, which was then crossing, was over. All this time the firing on the right became heavier and apparently nearer to us, our fears began to be aroused that the right wing was being driven rapidly back upon us. At this juncture...it became more and more evident that the right was being driven rapidly back upon us.

On and on they came, till the heaviest fire was getting nearly around to the pike leading to Nashville, when General Rosecrans appeared in person, and ordered me to go with my brigade at once to the support of the right, pointing toward our rear, where the heaviest fire was raging. General Van Cleve's division and Colonel Harker's brigade received the same order....

...I was moving my command from point to point, ready to support any troops that most needed it, the onslaught of the enemy seemed to be in a great measure checked, and we had reasonable probability of maintaining this line. During all this time my men were exposed to a severe fire of shot and shell from a battery on the other side of the river, and several were killed. About this time an aide of General Palmer came galloping up to me and said that, unless he could be supported, his division would have to give way....

...The line they were trying to hold was that part of our original line of battle lying immediately to the right of the railroad. This portion of our original line, about two regimental fronts, together with two fronts to the left, held by Colonel Wagner's brigade, was all of our original line of battle but what our troops had been drive from; and if they succeeded in carrying this they would have turned our left, and a total rout of our forces could not then have been avoided.

Seeing the importance of the position, I told my men it must be held, even if it cost the last man we had. I immediately sent in the Twenty-sixth Ohio, commanded by the gallant Maj. William H. Squires, to take position on the right of the Third Kentucky, and support them, and dispatched an aide for Estep's Eighth Indiana Battery to come to this point and open on the enemy. No sooner had the Twenty-sixth got into position than they became hotly engaged, and the numerous dead and wounded that were immediately brought to the rear told how desperate was the contest. The gallant Lieutenant McClelland, of that regiment, was brought to the rear mortally wounded, and expired by my side in less than five minutes from the time the regiment took position; still the fight went on, and still brave men went down. The Third Kentucky, now reduced to less that one-half of its original numbers, with ten out of its fourteen remaining officers badly wounded, were still bravely at work.

In less than ten minutes after the fall of Lieutenant-Colonel McKee, the gallant Maj. Daniel R. Collier, of that regiment received two severe wounds—one in the leg and the other in the breast. Adjutant Bullitt had his horse shot under him, but nothing could induce either of them to leave the field. Equally conspicuous and meritorious was the conduct of Major Squires and Adjutant Franklin, of the Twenty-sixth Ohio. Major Squires' horse was shot three times through the neck; nevertheless, he and all his officers stood by throughout, and most gallantly sustained and encouraged their men. Estep's battery came up in due time, and, taking position on a little rise of ground in rear of the Twenty-sixth Ohio and Third Kentucky, opened a terrible fire of shot and shell over the heads of our infantry.

In about one hour after the Twenty-sixth Ohio got into position this terrible attack of the enemy was repulsed, and they drew back into the woods, and under cover of an intervening hill, to reform their shattered columns and renew the attack....

...the enemy emerged from the woods and over the hill, moving upon us in splendid style and in immense force. As soon as they came in sight, the Sixth and Twenty-sixth Ohio and Estep's battery opened on them, and did splendid execution. But on they came till with 100 yards of our line, when Colonel Buell, of the Fifty-eighth Indiana, who lost 3 men, but had not fired a shot, ordered his men to fire. The effect was indescribable. The enemy fell in windrows, and went staggering back from the effects of this unexpected volley....

...The Fifty-eighth Indiana having now been over three hours in action, and the Twenty-sixth Ohio about four hours, were exhausted and very nearly out of ammunition. I, therefore, relieved the Fifty-eighth Indiana with the Fortieth Indiana, from Colonel Wagner's brigade, and the Twenty-sixth Ohio was relieved by the Twenty-third Kentucky. There was now not more than an hour of day left....

The brigade went into action with 71 officers and 1,454 enlisted men and lost—officers killed, 4; wounded, 21; enlisted men killed, 42; wounded, 278; missing, 34. Total killed wounded and missing in brigade, 379....

During the evening of the 31st I was notified that, in consequence of the indisposition of General Wood and a wound received during the day, he was relieved of the command of the division, and that the same would devolve upon myself.

The line of the division was nearly at right angles with the railroad, with the center of the line resting on it—the First Brigade, Colonel Buell [includes the 26th Ohio] on the right; the Third, Colonel Harker, in the center, and the Second, Colonel Wagner, on the left.

In this position we lay all the next day, January 1, with nothing more to break the silence than picket firing and an occasional artillery duel. The division lost, however, several killed and wounded during the day....

We maintained this position during the night of the 1st, and till about 8 o'clock in the morning of the 2d, the battery occupying the intervals between brigades. At this time the enemy opened upon us the most terrific fire of shot and shell that we sustained during the entire engagement. It appears that during the night before they had massed and masked several batteries in our front, so they opened on us from a line of batteries one-quarter of a mile long, all at once. They had our range perfectly, so that their fire was terribly effective from the first.... After about half an hour this firing ceased....

...I received an order from General Crittenden to cross with my division, and immediately put the different brigades in motion. While crossing at the ford, one or two pieces of the enemy's artillery were playing upon us, but it was then dusk, their firing was not accurate, and I think we sustained no loss in crossing....

General Davis and myself then fortified our fronts as well as we could with the logs, stones, and rails at hand, and remained in this position that night, the next day (January 3), and till about 12 o'clock that night, without anything other than picket firing transpiring. I should remark that it rained very hard all day of January 3, and during the night, so our men and officers suffered severely.

The division went into action with 254 commissioned officers and 4,633 enlisted men, and lost—officers killed, 11; officers wounded, 56; enlisted men killed, 200; enlisted men wounded, 859; enlisted men missing, 167. Total killed 211; wounded, 915; missing, 167. Total killed, wounded, and missing in the division, 1,293.

MILO S. HASCALL
Brigadier-General of Vols
Comdg First Division, Left Wing

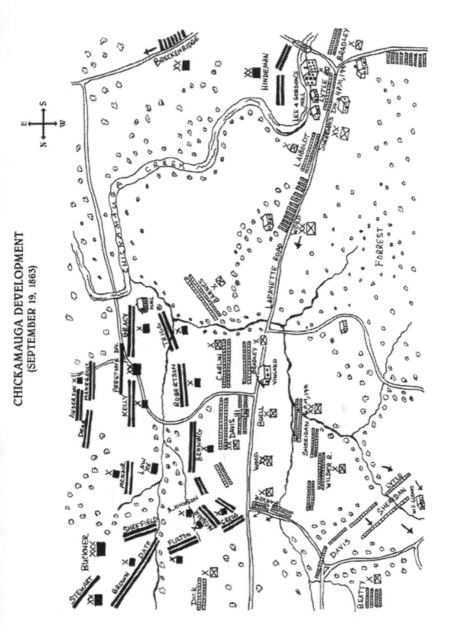

CHICKAMAUGA DEVELOPMENT
(SEPTEMBER 19, 1863)

10.

"...for this thy brother was dead, and is alive again; and was lost, and is found." Luke 15:32

During the first half of 1863, General Braxton Bragg's Confederate Army of Tennessee tore at the exposed flesh of General William Rosecrans' Army of the Cumberland whenever advantage surfaced. Tullahoma, Unionville, Shelbyville, Bradyville, Middleton and Hoover's Gap, Tennessee, among other chance locations, saw brief yet intense brawls. Even so, throughout the summer Jonah did not question the Union Army's seeming lack of strategy.

The debilitating self-analysis that had infected Jonah's life drifted away like an echo in a cavern, supplanted by the simple truth that all humans, whether they like it or not, live only one day at a time. He was promoted to sergeant in April, and when General Bragg began his well-organized retreat toward Chattanooga in July, Sergeant Hommen and the 26th Ohio, still a part of the Army of the Cumberland, followed cautiously. The groundwork for Jonah Hommen's Chickamauga ablution had begun.

In August, Union General Ambrose Burnside tramped his Department of the Ohio troops south from Lexington, Kentucky, toward Knoxville, and General Rosecrans, still in Central Tennessee, attempted a pincers movement with him. But Rosecrans, sensing that Bragg had at last panicked and might escape, leapt forty miles straight southeast from Tullahoma, hot on his adversary's heels, while Burnside simply settled into Knoxville to watch.

Bragg withdrew toward Chattanooga strongly reinforced by Georgia militia coming up to join him, To further support his battle plan, he summoned Confederate General Longstreet's seasoned divisions from the East, which turned out to be a pioneer movement by rail. Bragg then abandoned Chattanooga, moving even further south into the north Georgia hills. Rosecrans, scrambling to snare his fleeing quarry, split his main force into three groups, hoping one of them would engage the Confederate general before he could escape, and then all three could unite to defeat him. But escaping was not on the Rebel general's agenda. Instead, he consolidated his forces in the rough country south of Chattanooga and prepared for a decisive stand.

Bragg had designed a clever trap, a bold stratagem worthy of Napoleon Bonaparte-divide then conquer-and Rosecrans had unwittingly helped him achieve his aims. The stage was set for one of the bloodiest battles of the entire Civil War.

Rosecrans, finally realizing that Bragg had stopped retreating, ordered his outnumbered and divided Union forces, spread over forty miles of Georgia mountain country, to begin regrouping on General Thomas' XIV Corps. On September 18 he had nearly fused his forces, in spite of enemy cavalry slowing his consolidation by ambushing the amalgamating troops, which added to the confusion of the hasty convocation.

Well equipped for sustained operations and ready for combat, the eager Union commanders became sick to death of their terrain-blinded scramble, an order obviously intended for them to find safety in each other's company. But, realizing the urgency of the situation, they continued to demand prolonged effort from their material-laden soldiers. By the time the 58,000 tired Federals finally packed themselves into three square miles around Lee and Gordon's Mill on north Georgia's Lafayette Road, few doubted that the inevitable fight was imminent.

For eight days the Confederate Army had maneuvered through the north Georgia hill country trying to get a clear whack at the enemy, and on Friday, September 19, 1863, they did. During the next two days and nights, 28,218 men would die or be seriously wounded along a few miles of densely wooded creek called Chickamauga, The River of Death according to the ancient Cherokee Indians who named it.

Chickamauga Creek wends its way north to the Tennessee River through a five-mile-wide valley laced with snaking gullies and low rolling ground; the dense stands of deciduous timber, pines, creeping vines and bushes of every description defy timely movement, especially along the creek beds and in the lowlands. On the eighteenth day of September, the 26th Ohio Infantry Regiment, now commanded by Lieutenant Colonel William H. Young, camped in a rare clearing along Chickamauga Creek where it approaches Lafayette Road, a main passage south into Georgia over Missionary Ridge.

The regiment had become a part of Colonel George P. Buell's Brigade, Wood's Division, Crittenden's Corps, and the brigade, usually deployed as a unit, was, in addition to the 26th Ohio, composed of the 100th Illinois Infantry, 13th Michigan Infantry, 58th Indiana Infantry, and the 8th Indiana Artillery Battery, a formidable force soon to be reorganized by the Rebels. Colonel Buell's Brigade mustered a total of 1,821 foot soldiers and 134 artillerymen, who wielded two 12-pound Napoleon howitzers and four six-pounders. In the next two days, six hundred forty-eight men, over one-third of the brigade's strength, would be lost.

Early the next morning, the nineteenth of September, while Colonel Buell's Brigade relaxed at Lee and Gordon's Mill on the Lafayette Road, Jonah routinely prepared his men for the approaching battle, as did most of the brigade's infantry sergeants. At the same time, unknown to Buell, Rebel Generals Polk and Longstreet were advancing their forces into the eastern reaches of Chickamauga Creek, only a few miles northeast from his breakfasting brigade. General Bragg planned to sever the Yankee's lines of communication to Chattanooga and then crush them. Five miles north of Lee and Gordon's Mill, Rebel General Nathan Bedford Forrest's dismounted cavalry began to cross the creek at Reed's Bridge, to the surprise of General Thomas' soldiers relaxing in tangled woods opposite, a cedar thicket three miles long and over a mile deep. By alerting the enemy in front of him, Forrest unknowingly drew together the two armies. The battle had begun.

Soon after Forrest crossed Reed's Bridge, a solid line of yowling Rebel skirmishers broke into the one-hundred acre field lying just east of the Viniard House on the Lafayette Road, only one mile north of Sergeant Hommen and Colonel Buell's Brigade. Union and Confederate skirmishers blistered each other in the open field, then the Rebels turned and ran full bore for the safety of their own forces coming up in the timber behind them. The advancing Southerners met and faced off against the men of Carlin's Brigade, Davis' Division, McCooks' Corps, who quickly began digging in along Lafayette Road.

At eleven o'clock, Jonah and the soldiers of Buell's Brigade hurled themselves into the battle line on the left flank of Carlin's Brigade at a sustained doublequick, the Viniard farmhouse behind them, their cannon swinging in next to them on their right. The reinforcing Yankees jammed themselves elbow-to-elbow along a lightly wooded strip on the west side of Lafayette Road, watching the main Rebel body, firing steadily, surge out of the dense woods to the east and pour into the field in front of them. The determined Rebels had started a powerful thrust calculated to annihilate anything that stood in their way.

. . . . .

That morning, the unusually crisp air stroked Sergeant Hommen as he crawled from his tent at Lee and Gordon's Mill. He looked up and smiled into the gathering light under a cloudless sky. Although summer's final days had become pleasantly warm quite early in the day so far, today the autumnal forest seemed reluctant to shake off the early morning chill. Overhead, many brittle, sap-starved leaves still clutched their ebbing lifeline, seeming to tremble in fear of the breeze that would soon send them fluttering to the ground. Swift nightfalls now foreshadowed the coming winter–an ominous portending for men-at-arms in the field. And in three days the plunging sun would once again hover over the equator at its descending equinox, signaling the official end of life for Georgia's autumnal landscape. For many soldiers now on the cusp of battle, death would come sooner—Chickamauga's quiet woods and fields would witness a transformation outside the realm of nature.

Soon after the regimental bugle shattered the early morning stillness, Jonah rousted his troops and began helping them strike tents and load the rolled canvas into wagons. After a hurried breakfast, he formed his twelve men in the warming sun and began his routine equipment check.

At first, the new men resented Jonah's daily inspection of open ammunition boxes and haversacks, thinking it a compulsive excess on his part, but the veterans, knowing the price leaky cartridges might have in battle, accepted their sergeant's methods. The occasional gripe hid the fact that new and old soldiers alike knew each man depended on his comrades in the fight, experienced or not.

Jonah took his time as he walked behind his squad of men, looking into each black case to confirm a full load of Minié balls, eyeing their smooth, gray, innocent cast, for a moment remembering the deadly slugs' airborne scream and heated impact that often smashed the soft lead into a ripping shard.

He dismissed his men to await movement orders, but the image of deadly gray Minié balls and powder cartridges lingered. Like people, soft lead has flaws, he realized, its nicks tearing the air, groaning a warning. Mind the noise, he mused…if you can hear it, it will not harm you. Signing his muster slip, he again smiled. The entire company had gathered in the warming sunshine on the edge of the cleared campground. Jonah strolled toward the waiting men.

After Jonah's promotion to sergeant the previous April, recruits as well as veterans had learned to respect his confident soldiering and steady, pleasant manner. The new men instinctively sought his company, seeking words of wisdom. On those occasions, Jonah and the other veterans exchanged faint, understanding smiles, saying little. The survivors of Stones River had achieved a humble certainty in their soldiering, a thing they once searched for in the men who had escaped the meat grinder at Shiloh Church. They now understood that their metamorphosis could not be passed to the new men with mere words; each must find self-reliance his own way, in his own time. Sergeant Vieland, Jonah realized, had spoken the truth.

John Shoemaker broke the early-morning stillness

surrounding the waiting men, snapping a few heads around:

"Well, lookee thar! Venison on the hoof," he drawled, pointing to a deer that had run recklessly into the clearing.

"Not much doubt about what's scarin' the critter," Cole added, quickly exhausting his self-imposed word allowance. The men watched the big buck throw back its head and ricochet into the woods.

"That animal could'a been a Secesh scout," Fry said, his drooping mustache spreading into a grin, "since the rascal lit out like his tail was afire when he seen us." Fry's comment brought a few weak chuckles.

They watched two more deer bound from the woods and prance in blind panic over the open ground where their tents had stood, heads held high, bulging eyes flashing. The experienced men knew what had frightened the deer, scaring them into the open field, and it was not the Southerners' Walker dogs leading a deer hunt.

Suddenly an officer, his horse's eyes as wide as the terrified deers', came at full gallop down Lafayette Road, leaping from his roan before the horse could stop. The officer stumble-ran into the command Sibley while an orderly chased down his mount.

In a few minutes, Colonel Young burst from the command tent roaring *"Fall in on the road!"* His order, repeated by the company officers in sharp, echoic barks, cracked over the lounging soldiers like the whip of a mule skinner. Hundreds of men instantly broke from their campgrounds onto Lafayette Road, a swarm of ants unnested by the thrust of a stick. Captain Ross swung onto his horse, his saber flashing in the morning sunlight as he drew it in a circle above his head. Company C quickly formed on him.

The brigade's leading regiment, the 13th Michigan,

started to move out four abreast at the doublequick. Behind them the brigade began to surge like a wakened snake uncoiling, first stretching then slowly compacting as it accelerated north in the brilliant sunlight. Sensing its prey, the hungry Union viper twisted for a striking position, its deadly venom hidden in a thousand pouches.

Over his men's rhythmic thumps and grunts, Jonah heard the staccato bursts of random musket fire in the distance, fitful slashes signaling a surprise encounter. As the brigade punched itself up a slight rise just south of the Viniard farm, the erratic musketry fell to coordinated volleys, and then cannon cut loose, their thunderous concussions cuffing the column, tingling fingers and tightening stomachs.

Jonah's mind slowed, his concentration intensified; everything he saw became sharply focused in his tunneled vision. His body transformed into a machine that knew only instinctive action and reaction. The last undisciplined idea streaking through his brain was the fleeting thought that the fight might end before they arrived. It did not.

Colonel Young, his sword held steadily against his horse's flank, galloped past Jonah to the head of his regiment. Running full-bore just behind the company guide-on, Jonah saw the colonel wheel, point his blade toward the forming battle line. Above the swelling cacophony, he heard him roar to his mounted captains:

"*On the batt'ry's left!*"

Jonah did not wait for Captain Ross's order.

"*Left a the guns!*" he thundered back into the bounding mass of men, simultaneously leaping ahead to lead their blind momentum beyond the battery. The surging rumble of tons of equipment, horses and men hurling themselves into line of battle muted the snarl of Rebel lead tearing the air above their heads. Then, as if on cue, everything stopped moving and a screaming silence hovered over the men, broken only by the intermittent snorts of horses being led to the rear. The soldiers lay gazing across Lafayette Road into the Viniard field.

Through the lingering dust and smoke, Jonah fixed on a solid line of Confederates two hundred yards in front of him. Beyond them he saw still more scrambling from the dark woods bordering the far side of the field. As he watched, the first rank of oncoming Rebels fired another coordinated volley that thudded into the dirt in front and screeched through the air above. He lurched to the kneeling position and capped his ready load, as did John Shoemaker and Elias Cole on either side of him. Before they could fire, a twelve-pound howitzer at their right rear erupted, lashing dirt and debris into them. The blast rocked Jonah forward, leaving a piercing ring, but he steadied, fired and swung his musket butt down, in the same motion snapping the ramrod free.

Reloading by feel, he squinted straight into the sea of howling Rebels one hundred-fifty yards beyond Lafayette Road, their peals stinging his flesh. The waves of enemy billowed forward at the rout step, their solid front unwavering, floating at him like a curtain of rain carried on a steady wind. The tide of sun-danced gray, butternut and motley swallowed the open ground, almost a natural thing, spreading over the field like a blanket of wildflowers after a spring rain.

But their purpose was to kill him, and now they filled the field and still poured from the far timber. He watched the Rebel line hesitate as it absorbed a searing Federal volley, and then he sprang to his feet with the others, ready to burn the bastards again and counterattack. Vieland's words washed through him, a lifesaving mantra–*low...low...shoot low! Low...low...shoot....*

In one flowing action he squeezed off a well-placed round from the standing position and rammed another ball for the charge. Suddenly his left leg pitched backward, his heel smacked his buttocks like a whip, and his mouth flew open, snapping wide in a soundless scream. His left foot swung back to the dirt, but the leg could not support him. Before he realized what had happened, another shot smashed into his left thigh, spinning him around in mid-air.

Jonah slammed to the ground on his back feeling no pain, only a numbing wave sweeping through his body. He searched left and right and saw Federal cannon withdrawing, their seasoned crews swabbing, loading and firing as they backed away. Then the entire Union line collapsed to the rear, leaving him and scattered soldiers lying where they fell.

Jonah fished his belted skinning knife from under him and sliced his pant leg, exposing a gaping calf wound just above the boot. Staring at the ripped flesh he reached down and felt a splintered lower leg bone next to it, and then Jonah tore open his belt buckle, snapped free his trousers' fly and saw the minced meat of the thigh wound, then groped his buttocks in search of the shot's exit wound. There was none. He wrenched out his hand and rested it on his stomach. Sticky excrement pasted his fingers together.

Jonah struggled to roll to his stomach but could not. He managed to raise his head enough to stare between his sprawled legs. A Confederate officer galloped straight at him, his horse about to leap the remains of the Yankee battle line. Helpless, Jonah watched the bearded man lunge forward, his chest tight against the horse's mane, his left arm extended low under the animal's neck, gripping a sword pointed steady ahead. The Rebel twisted his wrist, sending the knuckle guard out, ready to thrust and spin-release as he flew past. Just as his Morgan's frothing haunches dipped and its forefeet swept up to jump the old line, a howling cannonball slammed into the animal's underside with a hollow thunk, the sound of a fist punching into a ripe watermelon. The ball ripped the horse's entire stomach away, throwing saddle and rider into the air, and warm, foul-smelling viscera spewed across Jonah as he watched, stunned. The shattering sounds and pungent smells of combat suddenly disappeared, and Jonah plunged unconscious.

. . . . .

He startle-awoke, the thunder of the fight still vibrating through him. He could see men in dark uniforms swarming over the old battle line, running east, their eyes on fire, paying no attention to the human carnage strewn across their path. As he watched, the determined Yankees drove the Confederates back over Lafayette Road and into the open field.

Jonah's pulsing wounds bled steadily. He had no way to check the flow. His left side had become a mass of dull, throbbing pain. He tried to move but sharp, spike-like jolts coursed through his body when he did. He had become desperately thirsty. He fumbled up his canteen. Something hard pressed his ribs and he reached for it. A tin of saddle soap had blown from the saddlebags of the eviscerated horse, whose ripped carcass now lay three feet above his head.

He sucked down half the flask's water and then pried open the saddle soap can with his knife, shaking a splash of water into the tin. He smeared the paste over his swelling wounds, nearly falling unconscious from the effort. The bleeding slowed but his turgid leg throbbed with greater force, sending waves of searing pain up through his chest.

Struggling to raise his head again, Jonah managed to glimpse his brigade withdrawing, falling back over him, driven unmercifully by an endless Rebel artillery and musket barrage. Yelping Confederates, wide-eyed blind in their frantic chase, flew over him and the dead horse; he clearly saw the ashen face of a young soldier as he flung himself to his knees next to him. The boy loaded, fired, and their eyes momentarily locked. As the startled lad leapt away, a terrifying sense of abandonment filled Jonah, and he lay listening to the battle rumble behind him, unable to move even his arms now.

At twilight, Buell's Brigade once again stemmed a rout, regrouped and drove the exhausted Confederates back over Jonah and the road. He watched the Rebels retreat all the way across Viniard field and into the dusky forest beyond. Soon, the firing stopped as darkness closed in, leaving him lying behind the Union line.

He listened to the cries of the maimed until midnight, when at last orderlies carried him to a wagon loaded with wounded, on its way to the Dyer house one mile north. As the wagon moved out he fell unconscious, but its pitching plank-bed soon knocked him wide-awake. In the eerie darkness he listened to groans and moans of the men surrounding him, joining the chorus when a lurch rolled him onto his wounds.

Jonah finally found himself on a stretcher in the open yard of the Dyer house, where a dozen white tents had been set up to form a makeshift hospital, but as it turned out there were too few. He could do nothing but suck in the biting night air and stare at the dim moonlight coming through the trees. At three a.m. an orderly handed him a bottle of whiskey. He gulped four swallows and passed out.

Before first light he heard officers shouting urgent commands through the numbing ground fog, then listened to the sounds of wounded men being moved. The rustling plump of a tent collapsing wafted over him, followed by the thump of equipment being flung into wagons. His wounds had not been treated. The surgeons had been too busy tending men who had been brought in sooner. At first light, two boys finally lifted him into an open buckboard drawn by a mule.

He arrived at the tent hospital in Chattanooga at noon, where an orderly cut away his clothing. He looked down to see dark crusts covering his wounds. The surgeon at Chattanooga decided not to amputate, telling Jonah that his self-treatment and timely evacuation from the battlefield had been fortunate. Most of the stricken, Confederate and Union alike, he said, still suffered where they had fallen, without medical help. Delayed treatment and saddle soap emollient had worked to save Jonah's leg from the grisly limb pile at the Dyer house.

Unknown to Jonah, Union General George Henry Thomas' stand at Snodgrass Hill on Sunday had prevented the capture of nearly all General Rosecrans' army. The Federals squeezed through Bragg's poorly sprung trap and gathered at Chattanooga. The uncoordinated Rebel flanking strike, intended to sever the Yankees' lines of communication, had failed, thanks to General Thomas and his men. The determined general's stubborn resistance earned him a sobriquet, The Rock of Chickamauga.

Jonah, his wounds properly dressed at regular intervals, lay on a cot at the Chattanooga hospital gradually recapturing his physical stamina and emotional balance. But as the days spun into weeks, like the beaten Army of the Cumberland, he experienced a spiritual rebirth that transcended his physical strife. Both the Union Army and Jonah had escaped annihilation, and now, juxtaposed with their natural urge to survive, grew a new, unforeseen vitality–for Jonah, a strength rising from true human spirituality, something that had been hidden within, the thing binding him to the rest of humanity, a thing oblivious to the chaos of war and the quest for glory and honor.

In October the sick and wounded helped each other

settle into a permanent, clapboard hospital barracks. After the move, hunger gripped the patients, the Rebels having surrounded the city and cut off supply lines. The Union wounded once again felt a deadly force threaten their lives. Jonah thought he might starve to death.

Each evening while he lay on his cot in the crowded ward he watched the nurse close the windows and doors to keep out deadly "night vapors". The dark barracks grew stifling as men hacked and coughed, spreading colds and fever among themselves. If one got sick, everyone eventually got sick, and although two fever bouts seriously delayed his release, Jonah's strong constitution overcame the barracks-cultured diseases. Throughout the next five months, his steady organic healing mirrored his quiet spiritual transition, although those around him saw only his physical recovery.

Jonah kept his personal Armageddon at Chickamauga Creek close to his heart, unspoken, a rock-hard foundation for his new awakening. And to remind him of his deliverance from the gates of hell, the twisted Confederate Minié ball rode in his left thigh for the rest of his life.

. . . . .

Lieutenant Colonel W.H. Young's Report on Chickamauga

(Official Record, Vol XXX, Part IV, Series 53, page 667)

HDQRS. TWENTY-SIXTH REGT. OHIO VOL. INFANTRY,
Chattanooga, Ten., September 26, 1863

SIR: I have the honor herewith to report the part taken by the Twenty-sixth Regiment Ohio Volunteers, of Colonel Buell's brigade, under my command during the series of battles recently fought between the Union and rebel forces on and near Chickamauga Creek, Ga.

At about 2.30 or 3 p.m. of the 19th, when the brigade was ordered to the left on the Chattanooga road, my regiment took the road in the rear of the One hundredth Illinois, and moved with the rest of the brigade at a double-quick some 2 miles to where the battle seemed to be raging with the utmost fury. Arriving at this point, where the conflict seemed fiercest, and the enemy was apparently pushing back our lines, my regiment was immediately thrown into line at double-quick on the right of, parallel to, and about 40 yards off the road, the Eighth Indiana Battery being on my right, my left resting in the woods....

...I immediately caused my men to lie down and simultaneously received instructions from General Wood that the position must be held. Even while receiving his instructions, and before the men had been allowed a moment to recover their wind after the rapid march, it became manifest the lines in our front were broken and the enemy pressing them rapidly back. In a moment more dozens, then scores, and finally hundreds, of straggling soldiers came rushing through the woods and over my line in the wildest disorder and most shameful confusion, there seeming to be no effort to either check or control the retreat, and at the same time a most galling fire began to reach and take effect upon my men, though lying close upon the ground.

In the meantime, I was holding my fire until our own men should be out of the way, intending, when the rebel line should show itself, to deliver my fire by volley and meet him at a charge with bayonets (previously fixed). As I was about executing this intention, a mounted officer came galloping to the rear calling out, "for God's sake don't fire; two lines of our own troops are still in the woods." At the same instant I discovered a rapid fire enfilading my line from the timber on the left, most cruelly cutting my command. My horse fell under me pierced, as afterward appeared, with nine balls; my acting major was dismounted and wounded, and the rebel line appeared in front within 20 yards, advancing firing. I immediately commenced firing and ordered a charge, but the command could be only partially heard, and the charge was not made. The rebel advance in front, however, was momentarily checked and his fire weakened; but the battery on my right had already been withdrawn; a heavy line of rebels were already on my left, and rapidly gaining my rear, making it impossible to hold my position even for a moment longer except with the certainty of capture I reluctantly gave the command to retire across the road to the fence immediately in my rear. This was done in tolerable order but under a most galling fire, Lieutenant Burbridge, Company H, and a number of men being killed, and Captain Ewing, acting major, with perhaps 30 to 35 men, too badly wounded to get away, being left on the ground. This conflict was short and bloody, began at a great disadvantage, kept up with the highest heroism, and the ground only yielded when the bayonet had been freely used and defense had become hopeless.

On retiring to the fence to position No. 2 the regiment was in great part promptly rallied, though under a severe direct and cross fire and the loud cheers of the advancing rebels. From this position an effective fire was poured back into the enemy, and he was compelled to retire to the timber for cover. But now a most terrible fire was concentrated upon us, direct and right and left oblique, there being no support on either of my flanks. The officers and men conducted themselves most heroically; many of the latter and all of the former, particularly those of the left wing, to whom my attention was more closely directed, disdaining the cover of the low fence and defiantly receiving and returning the concentrated fire of more than twice their front.

Again the enemy was closing up on my left flank not 30 yards from it and rapidly gaining my rear. I still hoped, though I had not seen it, there was some support on the left, and, depending for support for my right upon a rally that was being made around some old buildings 250 yards distant on the prolongation of my right, as well as upon a few brave heroes scattered along the fence between me and those buildings, I determined to hold the fence a few minutes longer; but it seemed of no avail. There was now almost a semicircle of fire around us; it was growing hotter every moment; we were beginning to receive the fire of our own troops rallied in the ditch below us and in the woods beyond. The five left companies had lost from one-half to three-quarters of their numbers. The left center company had but 5 men left from 24, and one of its officers was killed. Lieutenants Morrow, Ruley, and Williams, each commanding a left wing company, had been cut down while most gallantly cheering on their men in the unequal contest. Lieutenant Platt, of Company G (the Ninth), though still commanding his company, was painfully wounded, and already too many noble privates had written themselves heroes with blood stains upon the sod. It was a proud thing to have died there with those that were dead; it was my duty to save the remnant of the living for still another struggle…. Many of my own men had rallied here when the line first fell back and were fighting bravely from the imperfect cover the shallow ditch afforded. From this third position another defense was now opened, and for a few moments vigorously and effectually maintained. But this line, like the others, was flanked and raked with a murderous fire. Many of the wounded were again struck, even the second and third time....

I immediately proceeded to reform my regiment, and after moving my colors into the open field, succeeded—with the assistance of my officers, conspicuous among whom were Captains Ross [Company C], Adair, Hamilton, and Acting Adjutant Grafton—in rallying the bulk of my surviving men.... ...we charged across the field under cover of Bradley's and Estep's batteries, but in the face of a galling fire. We were joined as we charged by many brave fellows who had staid in the ditch, and a few others who had remained by the fence. But here Captain Ross and Lieutenant Shotwell, both of the color company [Company C] fell mortally wounded, and many others less conspicuous, though equally brave, were stricken down....

...We drew back in tolerable order to the timber, when the regiment was again formed, mustering about 147 men out of 335 who had entered the battle, and 14 officers out of 24. Our ammunition was here replenished, and in obedience to Colonel Buell's orders, we were moved to a position in the woods near the road and on the right of the field in front of the road....

Immediately when all was quiet for the night, I detailed Lieutenant Foster and 10 men to go carefully over the battle-field and see that all my wounded were gathered up. He found many who had been overlooked by the hospital attendants and saw them carried away. Four musicians were wounded carrying off the wounded during the action....

Aggregate loss of officers 12 [of 23]
Aggregate loss of enlisted men 201 [of 354]

David Jardine

I am, sir, very respectfully,
W.H. YOUNG,
Lieutenant-Colonel, Commanding

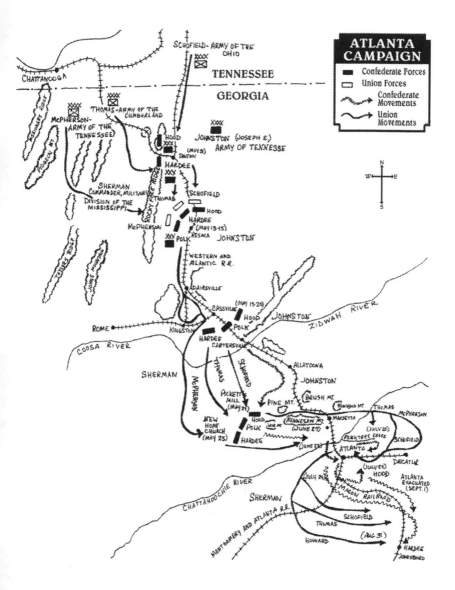

11.

*"But let a man examine himself, and so let him eat of
that bread, and drink of that cup."* 1 Corinthians 11:28

In late November, over two months after he was wounded, Jonah
still spent most of his time in the stagnant hospital barracks at
Chattanooga, lying on a straw-filled mattress and staring at
the whitewashed ceiling. The sharp odor of camphor pressed
him day and night, now and then overpowered by the stench
of infection or fetid gangrene when someone's bandages were
changed. He knew he had to escape the house of horrors soon,
but even now needed help to simply get on his crutches. Should
I request leave to go home and recover? he asked himself. But
how would I get back to Ashley without walking?

At first light on November 24, the rumble of battle began
to rock the hospital. The enemy had, since Chickamauga,
been digging in on Lookout Mountain and Missionary
Ridge, and now General Grant's able commanders, Generals
Sherman, Thomas and Hooker, were making their moves
against the Confederate strongholds. Jonah sat on his cot
listening to artillery barrages, wondering if his comrades

were in the fight. I should be healed by now, helping them win so everyone can go home, he ruminated. But what if I choose not to fight and request discharge? John Goodhue chose not to fight, back at Stones River. He showed the white feather and was killed for it. Why, he suddenly asked himself, am I resurrecting the analysis paralysis, a thing that nearly drove me crazy in the early days?

When night fell and the thump of cannon finally died away, he knew only two things—he could no longer tolerate the hospital, and he could not desert his comrades. He must walk again, and soon. Winter had tightened its grip, but with Spartan determination he began enduring painful hobbles to the chow hall for every meal.

The following Monday, after devouring a scanty lunch of dried beans and crackers, he returned to his cot and once again stared at the whitewashed ceiling boards, remembering the strong bond he had formed with companions still in the field. He needed to see them right away, verify that they were safe and confirm that the unspoken covenant they had forged in battle, one for all and all for one, had not been broken. But would they still trust him, accept him as their leader? Or would they look for weakness, signs that he could no longer be relied upon? Would John Shoemaker, Elias Cole and Sam Fry still have the stomach for fighting after Chickamauga? Would he?

That night, lying awake listening to the coughing and hacking of the sick and dying, Jonah suddenly realized that many of the other wounded men around him treasured the safety and comfort of the hospital, seeming to seek refuge in their infirmities. Was he doing that too? Was he hiding behind his wounds? He concluded he was not—the pain was too great when he tried to walk.

But he also perceived that he neither blamed the shirkers nor gave them credit for their clever deception. He had somehow learned to accept men as they presented themselves, not wanting to change them, not needing to change himself in order to be accepted. His compulsive need to judge others had vanished. In his darkest hour, Jonah had become willing to accept others as he found them, just as he had become willing to acknowledge his own humanness. And now he knew he must test his emancipation from the strictures of his needless social conformity and fruitless judgments as surely as a fledgling must test its wings. The decision brought a smile and he drifted asleep.

In January he began to walk fairly well without crutches, and in February he became a staff assistant, helping care for other patients. By the end of March he felt fit for the field, but the doctor refused to release him to his regiment until he could run one hundred yards without resting. In early April, insanely anxious to flee the hospital and rejoin his comrades, Jonah badgered the chief surgeon until he took time from his duties to watch him run. Jonah completed the test in record time. But his hip still would not pivot to full range, and his shortened stride caused a marked limp, which was obvious to all. Otherwise, Sergeant Jonah Hommen was fully fit for duty. The surgeon annotated his record and signed the release, sending him back to the 26th Ohio Volunteer Infantry. Although elated, Jonah knew that the physician was ignorant of the physical challenge a battle could generate, even for a marathon runner.

. . . . .

Jonah caught up with his comrades at Ringgold, Georgia, on the thirtieth of April, 1864. The regiment had been camped on a wooded flat along a small creek for three days, where he found his friends at dusk, eating supper around a smoldering cookfire.

Pausing in the shadows along the edge of their clearing, he stared at the men. As he did it all came back in a flood–

the years of campfires and hunger and sweat and danger and horror and death and closeness—and he grew numb as he stood quietly watching them. In the fading light their leathery faces and rough hands, chiseled by the relentless stroke and gouge of life in the field, mocked his barracks whiteness. He floated toward them.

"Well I'll be…," Cole muttered, half rising. His mouth fell open and beans spilled from his tin plate.

Shoemaker spun around and found Jonah standing two feet behind him; their arms jerked up simultaneously as if yanked by the invisible threads of a puppeteer. They shook hands without a word. But Shoemaker could not stop moving, impulsively seizing Jonah's shoulder as he searched for words, momentarily aphasic.

"What the hell…? Look at ya, ya…!" Their eyes glistened.

"I was only twenty feet from ya when ya got shot, when…," Cole murmured.

The others sprang to their feet in an emotional upwelling of loud greetings, and then, realizing the mindlessness of their reckless outburst, everyone suddenly fell silent.

"We been to Knoxville and back since Chickamauga," Shoemaker mumbled, confronting his aphasia head-on.

"I know, I heard," Jonah rasped, shrugging off his pack and bedroll.

"But our luck ain't been so good since ya been gone," Shoemaker added, chuckling, finally hitting his stride. "We almost cast lots to see who was causin' the bad fortune, like they did in the Bible! But the whale finally puked ya up! Our bad luck is over!"

"…out of the belly a hell cried I, and thou heard'st my voice," Jonah quoted, almost a whisper.

They laughed, an impulsive venting, but quickly recovered, realizing that their emotions might become an embarrassment again.

As Jonah moved toward the fire, the rest of the men rose to shake his hand, smiling, and he felt their respect, from some, admiration, flow into him. A young man who had not fought at Chickamauga said that of the 336 men in the regiment, 212 were lost in the clash, among them Captain Ross. Jonah sat down on a stump and sat rigidly, staring straight ahead. The men froze in silence, realizing that Jonah did not know the Captain was dead.

Cole snatched Jonah's mess kit from his pack and disappeared toward the chow tent. Shoemaker teased another log onto the hot coals. Jonah limped behind an enormous pine tree to urinate, and everyone watched his halting gate, but no one said a word.

"So, how ya been, Jonah?" Shoemaker probed when Jonah returned, smiling across the reborn flames. Realizing his faux pas, a blood-rush flushed Shoemaker's weathered cheeks. He fumbled up a tobacco plug and offered it to Jonah.

"Fine, fine, I feel just fine."

And he did. He felt pleasantly adrift among the familiar at last, but bone tired. He stifled an urge to eat quickly and find a private place to sleep. They sat around the fire talking for an hour, and Jonah once again felt admiration coming from the new men. He knew that the basis for their esteem was his wounds got in battle, the mark of courage, not first-hand familiarity with his soldiering. When he finally spread his bedroll that night he slept the sleep of a found child, in spite of his rising apprehension about how his crippling might endanger his brothers.

· · · · ·

General Thomas, the Rock of Chickamauga, now commanded The Army of the Cumberland, 61,000 men strong, and on May 7 led his force south along the Western

& Atlantic Railroad tracks. In the vanguard, Jonah and the 26th suddenly took fire from three cavalry brigades of Rebel General Polk's corps, men who had dismounted and secured themselves behind breastworks crisscrossing the face of a railroad grade called Tunnel Hill.

Rebel lead tore the air above Jonah, who lay with his men behind a sumac thicket. He turned to watch Major Peatman gallop back toward Colonel Squires, who was coming up through the woods behind them. Colonel Squires shouted at the Major, spurred his mount and vanished into the timber that still sheltered some of his regiment. Major Peatman wheeled, drew his sword, raised it, and when he swept it down the entire 26th sent a volley belching into the Rebel log pile on his signal.

Jonah tried to roll to his back to load his weapon but his leg would not propel him over. He lay on his side instead, shoulder raised in the air, and reloaded. After his second shot, Rebel lead screamed through the thicket, but once again he rolled only to his side to reload. He kept up with the others, realizing that he no longer must roll over, and, at some risk, had achieved a small personal victory in his first fight after Chickamauga.

He glanced back to see Union artillery batteries breaking from the timber, led by Colonel Squires. As soon as the guns found strategic positions their thunder began to cuff him. The Rebel firing in front stopped, and Colonel Squires, sword held high, galloped into the open. The infantrymen sprang to their feet. Jonah lurched forward, his men followed, and the chase up Tunnel Hill was on. As he ran he remembered the surgeon's one hundred yard test, knowing at the time it would be nothing in the fight, and it was nothing.

Polk's Rebel cavalry had leapt to their mounts in the face of the Yankee cannon, and Jonah, leading his men at the quicktime, chased them for twelve miles, all the way to Rocky Face Ridge in front of Dalton. There, Rebel General Johnston's entire Army of Tennessee waited for them atop the Georgia ridge. That night the Army of the Cumberland camped in front of the Confederate defenses, delaying their attack until General Sherman could catch up, his force twice the size of the Rebel army ensconced above them.

Clutching his throbbing leg, Jonah lay awake half the night before he finally drifted asleep. He woke an hour later, staring into the face of John Shoemaker.

"What you doin', John?"

"You moaned me awake."

"I hate ta say it, but my leg's killin' me."

"Try this," Shoemaker said, handing him a flask.

"What...?"

"Corn whiskey. They sell it on the sly behind the sutler's tent. Keep it, Jonah." Shoemaker crawled away into the darkness.

Jonah gulped two slugs and slid the glass flask into his haversack. He slept like a rock. The next morning he decided that he would visit the sutler's tent if it ever caught up with the regiment.

Colonel Squires held a dress parade on May 11, in full view of the enemy above. It was a pivotal event, apparently, because the very next day Rebel General Johnston retreated twenty miles south to Resaca.

The dress parade focused a few Yankee eyes as well. Jonah felt the weight of stares when his left leg double-thrusted with each step. But the men's lingering glances did not embarrass him. He now harbored an inner strength that seemed to repel criticism like greased leather shedding water. He nursed his emotional soundness, feeling it salve his soul. His hard-won self-honesty had begun to underpin his life with a certainty he had never imagined possible. After supper on the day of the parade, he moved to a remote clearing and lay down in the soft grass. His men quietly followed, saying nothing.

. . . . .

Unable to withstand the heat of General Sherman's strategic flanking movements, General Johnston left Resaca for Cassville, even further south. Johnston did not make another stand until his consolidated forces, now 74,000 strong, reached Dallas, where he built substantial breastworks. The Federals moved in to entrench themselves in front of the Confederate salient; the 26th Ohio faced a fifty-yard no-man's-land littered with blasted tree stumps.

Two days later, with a gathering summer storm at their backs, the men of Company C heard the regimental bugler sound the charge. Jonah lunged forward through the stumps, leading his men.

Smoke from a Rebel volley swept over them as they jumped into an abandoned trench half-way to the Rebel fortifications. Jonah peered left and right. On his left he saw the 49th Ohio charge forward, but before they could gain the enemy line a scorching volley thumped into them. Half the attacking men fell among the stumps. A torrential rain suddenly broke over the battlefield; when the storm ended nearly an hour later, Jonah crawled out with his men, but the enemy had abandoned their fortifications. The regiment reformed and marched forward, the red Georgia clay clinging to their boots. Jonah struggled to stay on his feet in the slippery mud.

On June 27, Kennesaw Mountain, a two-mile long, 700 foot-high ridge, rose in front of the entrenched 26th. The men quietly waited for the order to advance, while in the humid stillness, bright sunshine flooded over them with scorching intensity. Having insured his men were ready for battle, Jonah watched his sweat-soaked comrades search for shade in the angled log breastworks. Suddenly hundreds of Federal cannon cut loose behind them and the mountain came to life as Rebel guns answered the barrage, their shells bursting all around. The Union assault on Kennesaw Mountain had begun.

The 26th began scrambling up the sharp rise under withering fire, finally reaching the shelter of a rocky escarpment, where Captain Franklin, the company commander, finally stopped his men. Seventy-five yards to his left Jonah noticed that the timber had caught on fire, and as he watched, the flames swept down the mountain toward a brush-filled clearing littered with Federal dead and wounded. He leapt to his feet and ran toward the inferno, thumping a dozen men on the back as he ran. They followed him. The men broke from the trees and into the open field just ahead of the flames, and as they did, the firing, Rebel and Yankee alike, ceased. They began dragging the wounded to safety, out of the path of the fire. Rebels from the 1st and 15th Arkansas came from the woods and helped. An hour later the wounded were safe and the soldiers returned to their positions, and the shooting resumed with even greater volume. Major Peatman recorded Sergeant Jonah Hommen's humane action on Kennesaw Mountain in the Regimental Record.

On their bloody retreat south, the beleaguered but determined Rebels felt the sting of General Sherman's fury as he drove to surround Atlanta, the core of Southern industry. And General Sherman, confident in his military might and his larger social idealism of freedom for all men, fought hard to prove the rightness of his cause. But one of his soldiers, Jonah Hommen, struggled simply to confirm his own emancipation.

As the hot Georgia summer and Sherman's calculated thrust gained weight, many Federal veterans began to reach the end of their three-year enlistments. When asked to reenlist in early July, Jonah postponed his decision. Although he realized that it was time to go, for him soldiering had become the only life he knew and understood; the thing that made him what he was—severing military life from his psyche, he feared, might have the crippling effect of physical amputation.

On July 8 Jonah still wrestled with his decision to leave, and now faced the Chattahoochee River as well. Sherman's entire force had begun to cross, but according to Major Peatman it would be two days before the 26th took its turn. As Jonah watched Generals Schofield and McPherson lead their armies over the swollen river on pontoon bridges, he at last accepted the fact that he had also found his bridge over troubled waters, sailed through his personal storm, crossed the bar, and was home, free.

This time Jonah listened to his own inner voice, a thing he knew he must do from now on if he were to know peace, and his insides said he wanted to bring his liberated humanity home.

The following day he told Colonel Penwright he would not reenlist, and the colonel gave him a written order to go to Chattanooga for discharge. Although his comrades understood Jonah's choice, only Elias Cole, Sam Fry and John Shoemaker dared discuss his decision with him. The company had just finished towing two replacement float-boats into position with ropes, slipping and sliding along the muddy riverbank. They sat in the shade, waiting for the mud to crust on their legs so they could chip it away.

"You sure, Jonah?" Shoemaker grunted. "It won't be the same without you...like Knoxville, one damn mess after the other."

"It's time."

"It's *my* time in a month," Cole whispered.

"Six weeks fer me," Shoemaker added, "and I'm countin' the minutes."

The three stared at him.

"God bless ya, Jonah," Fry mumbled, and that was all anyone said.

In the morning stillness of July 10, 1864, as the regiment prepared to cross the Chattahoochee and march to Peachtree Creek, Jonah said goodbye and shook hands with his friends. The entire company watched him quietly strap on his gear and limp north toward a stand of timber hiding the Cassville Road. He glanced back and they waved. Jonah paused again, turned and stared at them for a moment, then swung toward the trees fronting the road, now burnished by the rising sun. He never saw his comrades again.

All horses and mules had been confiscated by one army or the other, the railroad tracks had been torn out and fire-bent by retreating Rebels, so only the Trudge and Tramp Promenade remained for homebound pilgrims. A supply wagon teamster going back for military stores gave Jonah a fifteen-mile ride, but the rest of the time he limped along, his sapling staff and halting gait telling his story without words.

For the next three days, columns of fresh southbound troops marched past, knowing at a glance that they saw a veteran sergeant on his way home. They waved, and a few shouted spirited slogans to show their tough-minded determination, but to Jonah they simply confirmed their own naiveté. The passing soldiers' rhythmic thrumps and jangles brought memories spanning thousands of weary miles on foot, but as they pressed south, the sequacious soldiers often missed Jonah's knowing smile, hidden by clouds of dust rising from their boots.

A cooling rainsquall swept the air clean as he crested Missionary Ridge on the final day of his trek, the refreshing shower sharpening his gratitude for simply being alive and free. He floated down to Chattanooga, his syncopated gate becoming a tranquil saunter through wet, sparkling woods.

He arrived at the city on July 18, bought civilian clothing at Uncle Jeb's Emporium on Market Street, and then reported to the army replacement compound on the eastern outskirts for processing. The sergeant major told him to be ready for discharge on the twenty-fifth. He settled into a clapboard barrack, and the next day rested, watching soldiers, mostly recruits destined to go south, paint the camp's wooden structures and rock-in muddy walkways. He and the few veterans awaiting discharge were not asked to work, but were left to themselves.

On the eve of Jonah's discharge, Sergeant Major Sackett, a solid, confident man that looked as if he might have been born wearing his thick handlebar mustache, found Jonah sitting on a hardtack box, busy retrieving his tin mess plate from his backpack.

"Care to visit town tonight...get a good supper, Sergeant Hommen?" Sackett asked. "Maybe sip a shot a big-city whiskey?"

"No, but thanks for askin', sergeant major," he answered.

Sackett smiled, turned away, and Jonah limped toward the chow hall. He knew that the top sergeant was curious about his war experiences, and sensed that war stories would inevitably find their way into their conversation, if they had one. But Jonah had no words to describe his struggle; therefore he preferred to eat his meals without company.

The next morning Jonah put on the gray broadcloth shirt he had found at the emporium, stepped into his machine-sewn dungarees and donned his cattleman's hat. He belted on a bone-handled skinning knife he had bought from a Kentucky recruit with part of his mustering out pay, then walked to the quartermaster's office and turned in his uniform, oil cloth, blanket, canteen, mess gear, and haversack. He asked the quartermaster for four day's rations, two more than regulations allowed.

Without speaking, the man left and crossed the street to the sergeant major's office. When the quartermaster returned, he said that Sackett had approved the request. Sergeant Hommen could keep his canteen, mess gear, oil cloth, and blanket, also.

Early the same afternoon, Jonah stood at attention in front of the company commander's desk, a Captain Wingate according to the plaque on the desk. The profound silence of the room pressed him, seemed almost alive, gripping him and the entire world. Sparrows suddenly began chirping outside the open window, loudly, as if they were sitting on his shoulder. He watched the captain scribble his name on the discharge papers, stand up and bolt outside as if the enemy were attacking. Jonah picked up his papers, and at that instant realized that he was no longer a soldier, no longer required to be anything except himself. He would never forget the moment and the feeling.

. . . . .

Jonah started north out of Chattanooga at three o'clock, skirted Signal Mountain, and at sunset the same evening limped through Walden, Tennessee. A half-mile beyond the village he veered into the woods lining the narrow road, found a clearing and built a fire for supper, a shrewd fire that the enemy would have trouble spotting.

He sliced beef jerky into a tin of beans, heated the mix and slowly ate, wiping the can clean with a biscuit. He buried the tin then sat quietly sipping a steaming cup of coffee. Gazing into the fire's flickering flames, Jonah remembered his comrades and wondered what they might be doing on a warm night in Georgia with the enemy close. They could be out on picket. He hoped that they, too, had a fire to comfort them, to stare and think into. He knew that campfire flames, even on a hot, black night in Georgia, held promise, giving a man hope.

Suddenly he heard voices, seemingly close behind him. He started to throw his coffee on the fire, but checked himself in time. Curious, he rose and idled through the woods toward the sound, finally spying a chapel nestled in the timber with dim light winking from its opened windows.

A dozen empty wagons and buggies filled a small clearing in front of the church. Jonah hitched himself into the churchyard, stopping next to an aging mare tethered to a split rail. Lonely and forgotten, the mangy black speckled roan looked old with her bowed head and bulging veins.

The resonant rumble of a preacher struck Jonah from behind, and he instantly visualized Reverend Sable. He turned to hear the welling peal of two dozen voices singing in harmony fill the still air, the hymn's guileless words coming right at him, piercing, as if he were the only human intended to feel their meaning:

> Aamaziiing grace, how sweeet the sound,
> That saaaved a wretch liiiike me.
> IIII once was lost, buuut now I'm found,
> Was bliiiind buuuut now I seeeeee....

He squeezed closed his eyes and tried to picture the singers, but the effort brought sparkling floaters instead. Opening his eyes he fought an impulse to go inside and see the people who sang to him in the dark forest. The soft light from the windows suddenly wavered, pulsed by shadowy movement, and then he heard the throaty preacher again, this time clearly:

"*My friends, the Bible tells us we be born sinful and unclean,*" thump, thump.

Drawn to the confident voice, he again wanted to go inside, but the brief urging quickly left. He need not be inside anything now. He smiled, turned, stroked the forlorn roan's flank and quietly limped away toward his smoldering campfire.

There were no people to watch his lame gait as he walked through the woods, no charitable, smiling eyes imagining manly scars got in battle. And it did not matter any longer, as it once did a hundred years ago, before Stones River. At his campsite he tossed a handful of twigs onto the coals, lay on his blanket and quietly settled into his own solitude. The holy chapel's hypnotic glitter winked unseen in the night behind him, hidden in the darkening forest.

In the slack silence he watched wisps of smoke from his fire lift into the cool evening air then twist into a thin, white shaft that climbed toward the sheltering treetops. There, the column hesitated, then crept through the fragile canopy, becoming a fleecy haze quickly dissolving in the silvery moonlight.

Jonah lay motionless on his back, listening to nature's hushed nocturne, and its peace flooded into him, and the weight of the day's burdens vanished. He slept without fear that night for the first time since leaving home.

· · · · ·

Major Norris T. Peatman's Report on the Georgia Campaign

(Official Record, Vol XXXVIII, II, 73, page 351)

HDQRS. TWENTY-SIXTH OHIO VETERAN VOL. INFTY.
Near Atlanta Ga., September 20 1864.

SIR: I have the honor to make the following report of the part taken by this regiment in the recent campaign of the army under General Sherman, commencing May 3, 1864, and ending on the 8th instant:

On the morning of the 3d of May the regiment, numbering 314 enlisted men, in command of Lieut. Col. W. H. Squires, left Cleveland, Tenn., and marched with the brigade and division in the direction of Dalton, Ga. Arrived near Catoosa Springs on the 4th and bivouacked there until the 7th, when we advanced to Tunnel Hill and again bivouacked until the 9th. Advanced on that day with the brigade to the top of Rocky Face Ridge to the support of General Harker, who after our arrival made a charge upon the enemy's works. During the charge the regiment was under a brisk fire of musketry, but met with a loss of only 2 men wounded. On the 10th commenced moving slowly upon the enemy and on the 14th and 15th had engagements with him near Resaca. Had 1 man mortally wounded.

On the 16th moved forward, and found the enemy at Adairsville on the 17th, and had an engagement with him. Loss, 13 wounded, 2 mortally....

...on the 19th [June] Lieutenant-Colonel Squires went back to the hospital sick, and I succeeded him in command of the regiment. Moved forward on that day some two miles... and halted in close proximity to Kenesaw Mountain.... Skirmishing was brisk during the night.... On the 22d had 3 men wounded, 1 mortally. On the 23d the regiment was sent to the skirmish line in front of General Kimball's brigade, when we were ordered to make a charge on the enemy's skirmishers, causing them to fall back to their main line. Losses that day 4 men killed and 9 wounded, 3 mortally.

June 27, we participated in the charge made that day on the enemy's works, occupying position in the second line of battle, and lost in killed 3 enlisted men and 21 wounded, 2 mortally. Lieutenant Foster, Company A, was also wounded. I was wounded myself in this engagement and was succeeded in command of the regiment by Captain Adair, Company I.

July 3, after the enemy had evacuated their works near Kenesaw Mountain, the regiment moved forward, with the column five miles, via Marietta. July 4, had some skirmishing with the enemy and built works for defense. Loss in the skirmish, 1 man. On the 5th marched to the Chattahoochee, near Vining's Station. Lieutenant-Colonel Squires returned from absent sick and took command of the regiment. On the 7th moved up the river about two miles, where the regiment was put on picket and remained until the 12th, while most of the division went on a raid across the Chattahoochee....

Very Respectfully, your obedient servant,
N.T. PEATMAN,
Major, Commanding Twenty-sixth Ohio Infantry.

12.

"For by one Spirit we are all baptized into one body, whether we be Jews or Gentiles, whether we be bond or free..." 1 Corinthians 12:13

The grizzled old man came out on the front porch of his clapboard farmhouse, squeezed against the winding road by cornfields, to see Jonah standing at his gate in the warm sunshine. A younger woman with two small children appeared behind him in the doorway, blinking into the early morning brightness. Jonah's canteen was nearly empty.

"Could I take some water?" he asked.

The elderly farmer stroked his gray beard then pointed to a covered well; the woman came out onto the tin-roofed porch but stayed behind the man, and the couple stood watching Jonah limp to the well midway between the house and the barn. He glanced back and caught the two toddlers peeking from behind their young mother's skirts.

He filled his canteen and hooked the ladle back on a rusty nail driven into the pump post, and then turned to them. "What's the best way to Crossville Tennessee?" he asked.

"There's a trail takes off half a mile north, on yer right. Saves ten mile or more," the old man answered, coming down the steps to point up the crooked road. Jonah hitched himself back out to the gate and the old man followed.

"Thank you sir," Jonah said, extending his hand. The farmer's vice-like grip surprised him.

"Yer welcome, son. You can be headed north or south, east or west, no mind to me."

Jonah suddenly realized that he now wore civilian clothes, that no one could know his political loyalties, and he had little need to know theirs for that matter. The patriarch spoke with a steady certainty; Jonah intuitively trusted the tough old fellow. He would watch for the trail–ten miles saved is better than a ride.

When Jonah saw the dark trace leading into the forest he hesitated. There would be no one to steer him through the tangled timber, guide him to Crossville, if he became lost. Trusting himself, he plunged into the woods, setting off along the shadowed path at a moderate pace, his knapsack and bedroll riding comfortably against his back.

Years of musket-toting, battle-equipped marching, often at an unbearable pace, gave his civilian rig a pleasant lightness, putting extra spring in his heels. Despite his halting gait, the feeling of being whole and sound seized him. The forest quickly swallowed him, Mother Nature tucking her innocent child into bed.

Pausing at a small opening where the trace widened, he looked up to see a crow sailing above the bright green treetops. The notion of the black bird's total freedom as it drifted over the countryside welled in his chest, and he plunged ahead, nearly floating down the trail.

In mid-afternoon he stopped under a spreading maple tree with amber-colored sap oozing from its trunk, then noticed a file of red ants scrambling across the sap run, using dead soldier-ants' bodies to bridge the sap run. The pungent smell of the natural mulch under his feet drifted up, and he lay down. His nostrils flared, his eyes closed, and he felt as if he were an inseparable part of the cool, quiet forest surrounding him.

Twilight and the Sequatchie River arrived simultaneously. After a quick rinse on a water-swept sandbar and a short firewood forage, he set up camp in an open patch between the riverbank and the trail. He had not seen a soul all day except the old farmer and his young family, and as Jonah kindled his fire, the thought that someone might be drawn to its glow crossed his mind. The sudden hail snapped his head around.

"*Hellooo!*"

An obligatory warning, the drawling call drifted from the trail just north of his campsite, in the direction of Crossville.

He stepped away from the firelight and searched the trees all around, then cupped his hands: "*Come on in!*"

Unsure of the moment, Jonah retreated to his pack that rested against a wind-felled tree trunk, thereby putting the fire between himself and the caller. He reached down and snatched his sheathed blade from the pack and tucked it under his belt at the small of his back.

Jonah watched a shadow flicker through the trees, seeming to flutter in the mirrored moonlight of the river. The gray, translucent gleam floated steadily toward the clearing like a ghost suspended above the ground in an effortless glide. The apparition finally reached the edge of the clearing where it stopped. The fire threw fitful glimmers over a lanky frame clothed in dusty, homespun garments, the fire's unsteady glow giving false motion to the man's solid stance.

The stranger wore a bedroll slung over his left shoulder that hung across his body to his right hip, where both ends of the roll were neatly cinched with a rawhide strip. A chicken dangled by its legs at the man's thigh, tied by the thong's loose ends.

"Where you headed?" Jonah asked.

"South…I got a fresh-kilt fowl here to share for the fire and the company, if ya like."

The stranger's deep, steady drawl seemed to frame every word he uttered, his speech the product of careful thought and a Dixieland boyhood, Jonah speculated, but maybe not.

"Done," Jonah said without hesitation, drawn to the stranger's open, trusting stance and straightforward manner. "Sit then."

"Been travelin' long?" Jonah asked, squatting to snap a stick in two and push the pieces into the flames.

"A few days."

"Same fer me."

His guest appeared to be an experienced traveler, carrying only a small, canvas pack, bedroll and canteen. The fellow swept off his soft-brimmed slouch hat, exposing his chiseled face, weathered from outdoor living but clean-shaven. His steady eyes sparkled in the dim firelight. Taking a step forward, the stranger shook off his bedroll and knapsack, dropping them against his heels. A worn pistol butt glinted from under the pack's overflap, and when Jonah glimpsed it he slowly stood, arching his back until his skinning knife's bone handle nudged his spine. He flexed his arm muscles, instinctively calculating the throwing distance to the lanky stranger.

"Name's Peter Trubody."

"Jonah Hommen."

The men stepped forward and shook hands above the vacillating flames, the fire dancing slivers of light over their half-hidden faces, intermittently eclipsed by the shifting shadows of their chins. They stepped back and the fire's hot embers suddenly flared, sweeping away the shadows and sending a rosy glare across their figures. They stayed fixed on each other, smiling.

Jonah sensed a natural decency and honesty in the stranger but, feeling vulnerable and cautious, he would not yet trust his first impression.

"Headed south too?" Trubody asked as he turned and bent to unlash the hefty rooster.

"No, no, north right now," Jonah clipped, squatting again, drawing another stick from his small pile.

Neither man had seen signs of travelers on the trail, washed clean by a rainstorm three days earlier, and without being told each already knew that the other had to be headed in the opposite direction. Had Trubody tested him with the question? Both men realized that it was risky to talk destinations without knowing intentions, and let the subject drop.

Jonah watched Trubody quietly spread his bedroll alongside a rotting stump at the opposite edge of the clearing. For several minutes the only sound was the sighing of the fire and the soft gurgle of the Sequatchie as it felt its muddy banks, groping its way toward the mighty Tennessee River.

Trubody came to the fire, smiled and swung the fowl over the blaze into Jonah's hand. Jonah spread the bird's wings, studied it, then laid it on the log and began to pluck feathers.

Having finished stripping the carcass, he started toward the river to slice it open and clean it. "Don't lose the gizzard!" Trubody called.

"Surely won't," he grunted.

Jonah cut a green stick, sharpened it, impaled the fowl and singed it over the fire. He then held the bird to the flames until it roasted, looking up to watch Trubody when he went to his pack for coffee grounds.

They ate in silence, speaking only once about the mild weather and the pleasant country they had seen along their respective paths. The war, a monster gripping the nation and everyone in it, lurked in the shadows, a menacing unmentionable.

"I'll stay the night if you've a mind ta share the camp," Trubody suggested, settling back on one elbow.

"That chicken was the finest I sunk teeth into since I don't know when," Jonah wheezed, struggling with a slug of hot coffee. "It'd buy a man more hospitality than I got to give."

"In that case, I'll do my chores," Trubody breathed, standing then walking toward the river. He stripped off his clothing, shook out his shirt and trousers and slipped naked into the river, cupping water from a shallow eddy pool and splashing it over his head and white shoulders.

"A wet man needs a good fire, a little warmin' from the night vapors," Jonah called toward him as he added wood to the coals. Attending to his own chores, he walked twenty paces into the trees to a huge oak and defecated behind it. Trubody dressed, and the men found their places across the fire from each other.

"Married?" Jonah asked.

"No. You?"

"No."

Silence.

"But I kept a woman wonst," Trubody added. "Hit turnt out she wern't that bright...got angry when she finally figur'd out I was smarter than she was."

"Why'd she anger over that?"

"Well, I wouldn't cotton ta her lame brain. You better show a woman you'll tolerate her empty rattle or she'll turn sullen an' saddle up."

"What if she's smarter than you are?" Jonah asked, chuckling. Trubody laughed and fingered a tobacco plug from his shirt pocket.

"Oh, that's fine, long's ya tell her how pretty she is now an' again. Sweet talk keeps any woman love-struck." He bit off a chew and handed the plug to Jonah.

Jonah felt the ease of fellowship in Trubody's humor, a relaxed sense of camaraderie. Their casual banter had somehow confirmed his intuitive judgment that he could trust this man, and a breath of serenity fluttered through him. Their eyes locked, and at that moment each knew that he could rely on the other, a seasoned soldier's insight.

"Done any farmin'?" Jonah asked.

"Some. Mostly sweet corn, cotton, beans, usin' some fer animal fodder."

"We raised corn, oats, and alfalfa for sale...then some acres of it for our own livestock. It's been awhile, though."

"Same fer me...awhile."

The men speculated about what the price of pork might be when the war ended, coming to the conclusion that the price would drop because of the lack of military sales. Then Trubody theorized that the vanishing need for military equipment and supplies might cause unemployment and drive city people into farm country, making matters worse for the veterans. But in their talk, each was careful to avoid giving clues that might lead to his involvement in the war.

Jonah gathered pine needles for his pallet, knowing full well that his guest had seen the face of war as he had, but also that the man had never signed a Federal payroll. Trubody, Jonah realized, had seen his Yankee canteen and mess gear and, apparently, accepted the implication. But had Jonah fully accepted Trubody without regard to his past?

As Jonah spread his oilcloth and blanket over his pine pile he became aware that, now that they had become friends of a sort, it would be difficult to use his knife on this stranger, maybe even anyone, for that matter. He wedged off his boots and settled to his back, stretching his muscles for sleep, the worn pistol butt hidden under Trubody's pack flap forgotten.

. . . . .

The gray, pre-dawn gloom gathered strength to confront the sun, a battle always lost, and in the heavy stillness of first light, the men awoke with a start, eyes snapping open as if by the same stroke. They had no mental catching up to do, no foggy reconstruction, no dazed hiatus between dream and reality. Mind and body came to life instantly, a warrior's reflex honed by pervasive danger. Each heard the other rising to his feet, but said nothing.

Jonah rekindled the fire, chopped and heated the chicken gizzard in the leftover fat saved in his tin plate, then soaked two chunks of bread in the warm grease. They quietly sipped coffee as they ate the chicken dumplings. Jonah wiped his mess kit clean with green leaves, rinsed it in the river, and together they rolled up their blankets.

While kicking dirt over the fire in the mounting light, Jonah studied the lanky Southerner carefully lashing his bedroll over his shoulder. Without a word they walked side-by-side toward the trail.

The men paused when they reached the trail, knowing that it was time to part company, most likely forever, and then stepped to each other. Their hands welded in a firm grasp, a fleeting smile sweeping their lips as their arms dropped. Saying nothing, they turned away and struck out in opposite directions, never looking back.

Twenty minutes later Jonah spied a barren knoll rising on his right and swerved toward it. To the south a vast expanse of forest came into view as he climbed the hillock. He searched for the small clearing that had been last night's campsite, where the trail almost touched the river, and found it. A thin layer of gray haze from their morning cookfire still hovered in the treetops, slowly melting into the windless sky as he watched. Beyond the clearing, purple shadows lined the winding river valley, their deep violet slowly paling in the growing light.

Golden sunshine swept over the barren knoll, quickly warming Jonah, and he could feel sweat spreading across his back beneath his pack. In the shade of his broad-brimmed cattleman's hat, his forehead creases grew moist. He fought an impulse to walk back into the cool forest and move on. Standing steady in the escalating brightness, he glanced at the sun, well above skyline now, then watched it slowly turn the forest's black rifts gray, and then begin to dissolve the shadows completely, unveiling a rich, green carpet of trees. He could not leave, not yet.

The forest's emerging pigments spread to the dense woods along the Sequatchie River, and as the valley's shadows fell away, the trees along the stream's twisting course turned first purple, then blue, then finally shades of jade. Awed by the landscape's natural harmony, he searched the river south, tracing its watery lifeline through the sun-drenched woodlands. As he looked left and right, the panorama's silent grandeur thumped into him, and he felt as if he were seeing his native country for the first time.

He stepped aside, cut a sapling for a walking stick and trimmed it, suddenly realizing that Peter Trubody did not seem to notice his limp. He tried to picture Peter among the many Confederate soldiers he had seen, in the many places he had seen them, alive and dead. He could not visualize Peter among the Rebels, and for a moment could not comprehend the connection, but he knew Peter had been one of the enemy. Peter Trubody had faced the devil war just as he had, and they both had survived. But it was over now.

The feeling that his suffering had now and forever

ended took away his breath, and he needed to laugh, or cry, but could do neither. Inexplicably, he cupped his hands around his mouth and shouted across the silent valley: *"I'm goin' home...I'm free...free...I'm goin' home free!"* His hands dropped to his sides and he drew a deep breath. His eyes began to glisten. A tear trickled from the corner of his eye.

As he started to turn he glimpsed a sparkle in the woods south of last night's campsite and paused. Standing frozen in a half-turn, Jonah tried to detect movement where he judged the trail might lie. Nothing. An impulse to scramble back, retrace the familiar path south and search out the compelling glitter struck him, and he smiled.

Suddenly he saw a black speck sail toward him from the shadows of a distant pine copse, a tiny airborne cross slowly growing into a soaring black bird. He watched the creature turn and float down to the river, its wings dipping now and then to correct its drift. It circled twice, finally alighting on the bare, bleached branch of a dead tree. The bird folded its wings, becoming a black speck again, but the brilliant sunlight began to wash its black sheen silver, melting the bird into the dead tree's sun-bleached branches. He stood staring at the white, naked tree, a chalky pillar guarding an emerald sea.

Jonah slowly finished his half-turn and stepped away, wending his way up the twisting trail through the silent forest—the best way to Crossville.

END